"Putting out fires is getting mighty old."

"Let me put out the fires." The words rushed from AJ's lips before she could stop them.

"Sounds like you think you can do that."

"*Yes, sir.* I can."

Travis narrowed his eyes.

"I mean, Travis."

He paused as if considering her words. "All right, then, let's go find Rusty." His eyes met hers and he smiled.

One smile and her pulse started a gallop that she fought to control.

When Travis nudged Midnight into a canter and took off toward the stables, she sat in the saddle for a moment staring at his retreating form.

For the first time, someone was giving her a chance to prove she could do the job. And it didn't hurt that he was smiling at the time.

AJ urged Ace forward, her spirit soaring as the wind whipped past. Travis Maxwell held her future in his hands. She'd have to be very careful he didn't hold her heart, as well.

Tina Radcliffe has been dreaming and scribbling for years. Originally from Western New York, she left home for a tour of duty with the Army Security Agency stationed in Augsburg, Germany, and ended up in Tulsa, Oklahoma. Her past careers include certified oncology RN and library cataloger. She recently moved from Denver, Colorado, to the Phoenix, Arizona, area, where she writes heartwarming and fun inspirational romance.

Books by Tina Radcliffe

Love Inspired

Big Heart Ranch

Claiming Her Cowboy
Falling for the Cowgirl

The Rancher's Reunion
Oklahoma Reunion
Mending the Doctor's Heart
Stranded with the Rancher
Safe in the Fireman's Arms
Rocky Mountain Reunion
Rocky Mountain Cowboy

Falling for the Cowgirl

Tina Radcliffe

HARLEQUIN® LOVE INSPIRED®

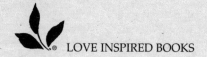

LOVE INSPIRED BOOKS

Recycling programs for this product may not exist in your area.

ISBN-13: 978-1-335-42819-6

Falling for the Cowgirl

Copyright © 2018 by Tina M. Radcliffe

www.Harlequin.com

Printed in U.S.A.

Trust in the Lord with all thine heart;
and lean not unto thine own understanding.
In all thy ways acknowledge him,
and he shall direct thy paths.
—*Proverbs* 3:5–6

Acknowledgments

This book came to life as the result of the prayers of the Sisters Writing Groups. Many thanks, ladies.

As with the first book in the Big Heart Ranch series, this book is dedicated to the staff and children of Big Oak Ranch. Big Oak Ranch is a Christian home, located in Alabama, for children needing a chance.

I'd like to thank Reba with the Pawhuska Chamber of Commerce for taking the time to patiently answer my email and mail me information on Pawhuska.

A shout-out goes to my newsletter subscriber Jo-Ann Toth, who named Travis Maxwell's mustang stallion, Midnight. Wonder Woman thanks goes to Rogenna Brewer (she knows what she did). Additionally, I would have starved during deadline if not for my very own hero, Tom, who gets a trophy buckle for outdoor grilling. The judges all give him an eight-point-five.

Thank you to my agent, Jessica Alvarez, for her wisdom and guidance. Thank you, as well, to my editor, Giselle Regus, who helps me grow as a writer, even when I'm certain I can't dig any deeper.

Chapter One

"I like Zeb Turner for the assistant ranch foreman position." Travis Maxwell looked across the conference table at his sisters, Lucy and Emma, hoping for confirmation, and then shoved another cinnamon roll into his mouth.

"Hey, you ate the last one," Emma said, grabbing the tin for the crumbs.

"I'm a growing boy." Travis patted his flat abdomen. He glanced at his older sister, who continued to scribble notes on a pad. "What do you say, Lucy?"

"Turner isn't even in my top three," she returned.

"What are you talking about? He passed the background check and the fingerprint check, and his résumé is top-notch," Travis said.

"That's true for all of the final candidates, Travis," Lucy stated.

"The point is that Zeb and I go way back. I can work with this guy and get the program off the ground and file for that grant. We'd meet the ninety-day deadline for that state funding faster than a bronc out of the chute."

Emma groaned. "Spare us the hyperbole, please."

"I'm telling you, my gut feeling is no to Zeb," Lucy said. "Now stop annoying me. I'm not feeling well."

"Lucy, are you all right?" Emma asked.

"Something I ate, I imagine."

"Excuse me, but with all due respect, Madam Ranch Director, I'm pretty sure the Fair Hiring Practices and Job Discrimination laws do not include your gut in the guidelines."

"Perhaps they should," Lucy shot back. "I asked you not to hire Rusty Parnell, remember?"

"I've written Rusty up and he is aware he's one boot away from being let go."

"Travis," Lucy said, "you and Rusty have known each other since high school and he's taking advantage of your friendship. Please, let's not make the same mistake by hiring Turner."

Emma clapped her hands to end the discussion. "Pardon me, but we have another candidate to interview before we proceed to decision making."

"Leave it to the Big Heart Ranch children's director to be the voice of reason," Lucy said.

"AJ Rowe." Travis glanced at his watch. "It's

bad enough Mr. Rowe went to the University of Oklahoma. He's also late."

"Now, Travis. Not everyone can be an OSU Cowboy," Lucy said with a laugh. "Let's not let our college rivalries blind us to a potential employee."

Heads turned when Lucy's assistant, Iris, stepped into the doorway. "Ms. Rowe is here."

Ms. Rowe? Travis mouthed the words to his sisters as he scrambled to search the candidate's résumé for a hint as to how he'd missed that particular bit of information.

He looked up in time to see AJ Rowe enter the room.

In a gray business suit with black heels, the woman looked every inch the professional. AJ Rowe had twisted her honey-blond hair into some sort of knot at the back of her head. She carried a black leather briefcase in her hand as she entered the conference room.

Travis did a double take. With those big blue eyes and that golden skin, the woman bore more than a passing resemblance to Travis's former fiancée. A woman who'd left him face down in the dust and had walked over him with her boots on.

His heart continued a crazy gallop as he carefully picked his jaw up, hoping no one had heard it slam into the ground.

Nope. This was not going to work. He was

looking for a combination rancher and bouncer. Someone to keep everyone in line, so he could get something done on occasion. The last thing he needed was a beautiful woman distracting him and his ranch hands.

"Ms. Rowe. We're delighted to meet you," Lucy said. His sister continued the introductions.

When Lucy came to him, Travis offered AJ a handshake, though he declined to meet her gaze, and he also declined to notice how soft her hand was.

"*The* Travis Maxwell?" the woman murmured with dawning recognition in her voice.

His head jerked up at the questioning tone and he connected with clear blue eyes.

"Have you two met?" Lucy asked.

"No. I recognize Mr. Maxwell from the cover of *Tulsa Now* magazine."

Travis bit back a groan. He'd been labeled Bachelor of the Year.

Lucy's idea, and he'd been paying for that particular bright idea in spades ever since the story ran last month. Women were still sending him emails, letters and had even showed up in person to let him know they would be happy to help him change his bachelor status to something long-term. The irony being that he had zero interest in relationships let alone matrimony. No. Been there and almost done that.

"Publicity for the ranch," Travis mumbled. He shot Lucy a death stare.

"He's only a part-time cover model," Emma said with a chuckle. "The rest of the time he's the ranch foreman."

Travis shook his head. Laughingstock of the ranch was more like it.

Once they were all seated, Lucy began a round of the same questions she'd asked the last five applicants.

Travis fiddled with his pen, glancing outside at the redbud trees waving in the breeze of an Oklahoma spring. The deep purple buds were open in an explosion of rosy-pink blooms.

He ducked his head to sneak a sideways glance at the candidate.

AJ Rowe gestured a hand. "I've been working ranches since I could sit in a saddle." Her voice held a trace of sadness. "My father was the foreman for two of the biggest ranches in Oklahoma in his time and I worked by his side growing up."

"You've got an impressive and lengthy work history," Lucy commented. "I can't help but notice that you've transitioned employers several times over the years."

"That's a nice way to address job-hopping." AJ smiled tightly. "The reality is that most ranches hire in favor of male candidates. Code of the

West." She shrugged. "If I am hired, it's short-term until they're able to replace me with a man."

Though Travis turned his head back to the window, the finger of guilt continued to poke at his conscience.

Awkwardness settled in the conference room. Finally, Lucy shifted the paperwork in front of her and looked to Emma for assistance.

"Tell us about your equestrian experience," Emma prompted.

"I've done quite a bit of professional barrel racing."

Travis glanced at the paperwork. "You didn't mention that in your résumé."

"An omission," she murmured.

Omission? Barrel racing was a female-dominated sport. Travis had no doubt that she'd left it off her résumé for that reason. That, along with the gender-neutral name AJ, would ensure she got an interview at very least.

So why did that annoy him so much? Because he didn't believe for a heartbeat that he had a bias and he didn't like being treated as though he did.

Another gap in conversation had Emma once again breaching the silence.

"I used to barrel race, too," his sister gushed. "Of course, I was never a professional, but I did compete locally. Are you still competing?"

"Mostly I train. I enjoy working with young

girls and teaching them to appreciate the sport. Healthy competition builds self-esteem, and the fact that they're focused on something other than boys is even better."

Both Lucy and Emma smiled. Mention children and his sisters were on board. After all, Big Heart Ranch existed solely for the children.

"That's wonderful," Lucy said, confirming his thoughts. "Interaction with our kids is a large part of the job. The children of Big Heart Ranch have backgrounds of abuse, abandonment and neglect, and they are, of course, our number-one priority."

AJ offered a sympathetic nod.

"I'm sure Travis has some questions for you," Lucy said as the toe of her boot made contact with his shin under the table.

He offered a weak smile. "What are your thoughts on cattle management, Ms. Rowe?"

"Bison." Her full lips curved into an excited smile. "Have you considered bison?"

Travis frowned and blinked with stunned surprise. "Bison? Ah, no. Cattle is the best choice for Big Heart Ranch," he said firmly.

"And yet bison have many advantages, including efficient feed utilization, low-fat and high-protein meat with an ever-increasing consumer demand. Lower vet bills. They're hardy and disease-resistant and calve without assistance."

Why was the woman still smiling?

"You've read the recent studies on grazing?" she continued.

"I have." He met her gaze head-on.

"Wonderful. Perhaps we could discuss other sustainability ideas I have. I mean, at your convenience."

"I, uh… Yeah. Sure." He faltered and turned to his sisters. "Was there anything else?"

Lucy closed the folder in front of her and stood. "I believe that covers everything. We're done here and, needless to say, we're very impressed."

AJ stood, as well. "Thank you, Ms. Maxwell."

"Call me Lucy."

The moment his sister clasped AJ's hand with both of hers, Travis knew he was in trouble.

"We're family at Big Heart Ranch," Emma chimed in as she, too, stood.

Travis grimaced and slowly got to his feet. He offered a nod of acknowledgment without meeting AJ's gaze.

"We'll be in touch by the end of the week," Lucy said.

Travis shoved his hands in his pockets and paced across the conference room as the tap-tap-tap of heels on the vinyl floor echoed down the hall, followed by the whoosh of the big glass doors as they closed behind AJ Rowe.

"I like her," Emma said. "She'll fit right in. The

woman has great ideas, too. We could use a little shake-up around here."

"Lucy marrying Jack Harris last year wasn't enough of a shake-up for you?" Travis asked.

"Look where that got us." Emma wrapped an arm around Lucy's shoulders. "Jack has provided the impetus for the new retreat center and both Lucy and I have our very own personal assistants."

Lucy narrowed her eyes at Travis. "I can't see any downside to hiring AJ."

"Maybe we should vote," Emma suggested.

"No voting required," Travis said. "I'm the guy who has to work with the candidate we hire. I get to make the decision."

"Clearly you have forgotten that all three of us own Big Heart Ranch," Lucy said.

"She omitted information from her résumé," Travis said.

"Information that would have only made her an even more impressive candidate for the job," Lucy returned.

"Come on, Travis," Emma said. "She omitted the information to offset bias. I get that."

"I don't need an assistant who can't do the job."

"You don't know she can't do the job," Lucy said. "Even you have to admit that her résumé is better than Zeb Turner's."

Emma nodded. "The woman can ride. She was

raised on ranches and has the education, plus the experience, for the position."

"But can she handle the ranch hands?" he asked.

"I think AJ Rowe can probably do anything she sets her mind to," Emma murmured.

Travis stared his youngest sister down. "What's that supposed to mean?"

Lucy sat back down and moved the folders on the table into a neat stack. "It means we want to hire AJ."

"I don't think you two understand what's on the line here. I've got a little less than ninety days to launch the cattle management program and submit evidence of a successfully implemented plan to the Oklahoma Ranchers and Farmers Grant Program. I can't afford to hire the wrong person."

"Travis, that grant is offered every year. There's no pressing deadline. Sure, we'd like to launch the program, but everything is God's timing."

"Are you kidding? I'm not going to let it go now. You don't understand how much this project means to me."

"Oh, we understand." Lucy's gaze moved from Emma and then back to him.

"This isn't like you, Trav," Emma said. "Are you sure this is just about the grant? Or do you have another issue?"

"I don't have any issues."

"Terrific," Lucy said with a nod. "Then it's settled. You know, I think AJ Rowe is going to be a game changer around here."

Yeah, that's exactly what he was worried about. He liked things the way they were. He'd moved past the uncertainty of his childhood and the shattered promise of what he thought was forever love, to life at Big Heart Ranch. With the upcoming launch of the cattle program, proving himself to his sisters and everyone at the ranch was well within his reach.

The last thing he needed was a game changer who wanted to put bison on his cattle ranch.

Travis shrugged and raised his palms in surrender. "Fine. We hire her. But let the record state that Travis Maxwell, ranch foreman, is conceding under duress." He slapped his Stetson on his head, turned on his boot heel and headed back to his steers.

A man could trust cattle.

Coffee. The aroma of good, strong coffee permeated the bunkhouse. AJ kicked the front door shut with the toe of her boot and dropped her saddle and duffel bag on the first empty twin-size bunk.

She glanced around. Giddy anticipation sparred with a still small voice issuing a warning not to get her hopes up.

There was a total of four beds. Two bunks were

empty, wearing only blue-tick mattresses. The third bed was neatly made with crisp, military-looking hospital corners. A thick quilt had been folded on the end of the bed. Diamond Patch. That was the name of the pattern of rich pinks and corals. She recognized it from the many her mother used to hand stitch. An open Bible lay on top of the quilt.

The bureau next to the bed held an assortment of the owner's personal items and a braided rug covered the nearby floor.

Home sweet home. Except it wasn't. Not for AJ. And she needed to remember that. Home was long gone and there was nothing left for her in Timber, Oklahoma, since her mother died. Big Heart Ranch was simply another job, another city.

When her temporary wrangler position outside Bartlesville had ended, she'd packed up her few belongings, gotten in her pickup and started driving. However her Chevy'd had a mind of its own and, just like her rodeo days, the truck had found its way back to Timber.

AJ opened her duffel and pulled out her own well-worn leather Bible and a photo of her mother, in a plain silver frame. She gently rubbed a bit of dust off the glass with her thumb and placed the photo on the oak bureau next to the bed. She'd left the rest of her personal things boxed up and sitting in the passenger seat of the truck, along with her interview suit.

No need to bring everything in because, if Travis Maxwell had his way, she'd be gone tomorrow. The man's expressive face during her interview had told her plenty. Travis was no different from any other ranch foreman she'd encountered, except the man was younger and easier on the eyes.

The mirror above the bureau captured her reflection and she stared for a moment. Her face was devoid of makeup, her skin covered only with a layer of sunscreen. She'd do whatever was necessary to fade into the background so Travis Maxwell would see her as a capable employee and not judge her based on her appearance. Gathering her hair into a severe low ponytail, she fastened a tortoiseshell clip at her nape.

With another quick look around the room, AJ tucked her denim shirt into her Wranglers, picked up her saddle and hat, and pushed open the back door of the bunkhouse.

A middle-aged woman with gray curls sat on the small porch outside with a cup of coffee in her hand. When AJ's boot hit the ground, she looked up and offered a warm smile. "You must be the new assistant foreman."

"Yes, ma'am. I'm AJ."

The woman glanced at her watch. "You're early. That's a novelty Travis will appreciate."

Confused, AJ opened her mouth and then

closed it again. Apparently a response was not required. The woman kept talking.

"I'm your roommate. Rue Butterfield."

"You're a ranch hand?"

"I'm a physician and a retired army general. I handle the health clinic on the ranch and medical issues with the children. Immunizations and such."

"Big Heart Ranch has a full-time staff physician living here?" AJ asked.

"Not exactly. I'm actually a volunteer and I have my own place in town." Rue shrugged. "Often it's easier to stay in the bunkhouse. Like last night. I was monitoring an asthmatic child over at the girls' ranch."

"I see."

"Don't worry, I'm tidy and mind my own business." Rue winked. "Heavy emphasis on mind my own business."

AJ couldn't help but return the smile. "Good to know."

"Delighted to have another woman around."

"Thanks. Um, is this a permanent women's bunkhouse?"

"Sure is. Why, Lucy Maxwell used to stay here all the time when things got busy. That is before she married Jack Harris and adopted triplets."

"Triplets!" AJ blinked, attempting to wrap her head around the information.

Rue nodded. "Emma and her twins have been

known to spend the night when the roads are icy between here and town."

"And I suppose you're going to tell me Travis has a dozen kids, too."

Rue laughed. "Not hardly. Although our Travis does loves children, he's highly allergic to relationships."

AJ didn't know what to say to that. She glanced at the road that led to the bunkhouse. "Can you point me to the stables?"

"You haven't had the official orientation? Met with human resources and all?"

"That's scheduled for Monday. Travis wanted me to start immediately."

"That's our Travis. Workaholic and then some. Even on a Saturday."

"Not a problem. I like to stay busy. Especially on a Saturday."

"You two will get along nicely then," the older woman said.

Thoughts whirled at the irony of the comment but AJ held her tongue.

"Where did you park?" Rue asked.

"In front."

Rue pointed to the black utility vehicle that was parked on the gravel. "Take the Ute. Keys are in the ignition. The main equestrian center is a quarter mile down the road, on the right. We have a smaller stable on the girls' ranch."

"Are you sure you want me to take the vehicle?"

"You're staff now, and the Ute is easier to manage on some of the dirt and gravel roads on the ranch."

"Thank you." She looked at Rue. "I have to admit, I'm not used to such hospitality."

"No? Well, you're going to find that things are different at Big Heart," Rue returned. "Love and the good Lord reign here. You'll see."

AJ couldn't help but ponder Rue Butterfield's words as she drove the Ute around the bend in the road. Was Big Heart Ranch different? The looming question was would things be different for her?

Ahead, a road sign indicated the equestrian center was to the right. She pulled the Ute into the gravel parking area and tucked the keys in her pocket.

In a small corral outside the stable doors, a group of young boys ranging from six to sixteen were being instructed by a young cowboy wearing a long-sleeved black T-shirt with the words *Big Heart Ranch Staff* on the back. Each youth took turns mounting a sorrel mare in the middle of the corral.

AJ tossed her saddle on the top rung of the roughly hewn fence and stood to watch for a moment. The scene lifted her spirits and brought a smile to her lips. She well remembered her first official riding lessons though it was the unofficial lessons with her father that were the most heart-tugging. Those were special times that she'd never forget.

"You found us."

Travis Maxwell. She turned around. He wore creased black jeans and a plaid Western shirt. The Stetson on his head matched his black hair. As usual, there was a no-nonsense expression on his beard-shadowed face.

"Yes, sir," she said, avoiding direct eye contact.

"Sir?" Travis shook his head. "Ouch."

"Mr. Maxwell?"

"Travis is fine." He looked around. "Got your saddle, I see. Are you boarding a horse with us?"

"No."

"No?"

What would be the point of hauling Gus all the way here? She had zero expectation that this job would last long enough to get her horse settled in. So as much as it pained her, she'd left Gus with her stepfather where daily boarding fees continued to accrue.

Thankfully, Travis didn't probe further and started walking in the direction of the stable entrance.

She followed, with her saddle slung over her shoulder.

"Let's see what's available," he said. "Most of the animals are on the schedule for lessons. Our equestrian manager, Tripp Walker, will assign you a ranch horse later today."

"Thank you."

He picked up a clipboard from outside the building and flipped through the papers. "Looks like Ace is all yours this morning."

"Ace?"

"She's a fine animal." Their boots echoed on the plank floors as they headed in. Despite the hour, the center was already busy. Horses whinnied and their hooves clomped on the stable floor as they were led outside. The soft crooning voices of riders grooming animals provided a white noise around them.

AJ peeked in past the gates of each stall, savoring the scent of animal and straw, pleased at the cleanliness of the premises. She inhaled deeply. Happiness did indeed have an aroma. This was it. The hay, the horses, the leather.

Travis stopped halfway down the center aisle. A chalkboard on the outside of the stall indicated this was Ace, a palomino mare with low white stockings on her forelegs. The animal's dark velvet eyes assessed AJ with interest.

"Good morning, Ace," she murmured.

The names Joey and Tim were also written on Ace's chalkboard.

"What does this mean?" she asked, pointing to the names.

"All the kids have chores. Joey and Tim are Ace's team. They do everything. Feed, groom, stall mucking and turnout. We pair up a younger child with an older one."

He pointed to an office, whose door was shut, lights off. The sign on the door read Tripp Walker, Manager.

"Tripp's the top of the food chain for anything to do with the horses. I'll introduce you when he gets in. He was on call last night."

"On call?"

"Yeah, and now that you're here, you can be in the rotation. We take turns being the point of contact for livestock problems after hours and weekends." Travis nodded to the right. "Here we go. Tack room."

Once they'd tacked up their horses, AJ followed Travis back outside and into the April sunshine. His black Mustang stallion nickered and playfully bumped his muzzle into Travis's shoulder.

"Midnight is spoiled rotten," he murmured. Pulling a carrot from his pocket Travis fed the treat to the stallion.

AJ bit back a smile. So her boss had a soft spot, after all. She found that oddly comforting. Maybe he wasn't all black and white.

"Let's ride the fence line. After today the schedule is all yours. You'll be assigning the chores, including the fences."

"Mind if I ask how many ranch hands there are?"

"Rusty Parnell and Dutch Stevens are my only full-time wranglers. Dutch claims to be about one hundred years old and keeps reminding me he's retiring in a year. He's been reminding me since I hired him five years ago."

"And Parnell?"

"Rusty is a piece of work, which is why I'm praying Dutch doesn't really retire."

"Two?" Her jaw sagged. "That's all?"

"There are also a couple of college students, Big Heart Ranch graduates. They live in one of the two men's bunkhouses and work part-time for their room and board."

"That's not a lot of help for a spread this size."

"Tell me about it. Hiring will be a priority real soon. Once we get the cattle program fully launched, we'll have our own student wranglers on board."

"What do you mean 'student wranglers'?"

"We're raising sixty or so children in family environments on Big Heart. The ranch is their home, which means they get the awesome privilege of contributing to managing the place. Helps them understand the value of a strong work ethic."

"Girls will be assigned, too?"

"Yeah." Travis paused, his eyes steely. "Girls, too."

Gaze unwavering, AJ refused to back down. After all, he was the one who had a problem with females, not her.

Silence stretched for a moment before Travis nodded toward the administration buildings in the distance. "Stop by HR on Monday. They've got a phone contact list and maps and all sorts of boring paperwork and classes for you that explain how everything works around here."

"Will do."

AJ's glance swept the buildings around the stables. "Where are the men's bunkhouses?"

He raised a gloved hand and pointed. "Behind the equestrian center. My office is in that barn. It holds tools and equipment, as well."

"How do I reach you? I mean, if I need to?"

Travis moved the stallion's reins to his left hand, reached into his back pocket and pulled out his wallet. He handed her a business card.

When their fingers touched, AJ stepped back, startled at the connection. The card fluttered to the dusty red dirt. She bent to retrieve the card at the same time as Travis. It was only his hand on her arm that prevented a full collision.

"Whoa," he murmured.

"I…" Tongue-tied and overwhelmed with awareness, AJ froze. Travis's dark eyes were round with intense scrutiny. She didn't look away.

A woman working in a man's world knew how to shut the door to a man's assessing glance. Why did she find herself hesitant to close the door on this particular man? Heat warmed her face as she chastised herself.

"I've got this," Travis said.

Her heart continued to trip wildly as she took the card he handed her, using care to avoid contact this time.

"Ready?" he asked.

AJ slid her boot into the stirrup and heaved up into the saddle. She followed Travis and Midnight through the stable yard and onto a well-worn path.

A cool spring breeze stirred the air, bringing with it the scent of Oklahoma red clay, grass and a familiar fragrance.

"Lilacs," she murmured.

"Yeah, Lucy and Emma planted dozens of them." He stopped Midnight and gestured to the left. "Over there by the pond."

"Why so many?"

"Our mother loved lilacs."

"You lost your mother? I'm sorry. I didn't know."

"We lost both of our parents. The three of us ended up in foster care. Lucy was ten, I was eight and Emma was five. That's the reason we started the ranch."

"I wasn't aware."

"They'll give you a history lesson on Monday." He urged Midnight ahead as if to indicate the topic was closed.

AJ did her best to keep up with Travis's more spirited animal. "The ranch is about five hundred acres?" she asked as she caught up.

He nodded. "Yeah, most of that is grazing land."

"How many head?"

"Fifteen. The goal is to triple that. We're looking to be self-sustaining and hopefully take some product to market after they feed for a year. Grassfed cattle are in demand right now."

"Do you live on the ranch?" she asked.

"That depends on what's going on. Nothing worse than getting home and having to turn around and come back to put out fires." He looked at her and pushed his Stetson to the back of his head. "That's where you come in."

"I'm here to make your life easier," she said.

"So they tell me." Travis's phone rang and he pulled it out. "Maxwell." He released a sound of frustration as he listened and then slipped the cell into his shirt pocket. "I've got a missing ranch hand."

"Missing?"

"Normally, this is Rusty's day off, but he volunteered to lead an early morning trail ride. He's a no-show." With a disgusted shake of his head,

Travis turned his horse around. "Putting out fires is getting mighty old."

"Let me put out the fires." The words rushed from her lips before she could stop them.

"Sounds like you think you can do that."

"Yes, sir. I can."

He narrowed his eyes.

"I mean, Travis."

He paused as if considering her words. "All right, then, let's go find Rusty." His eyes met hers and he smiled.

One smile and her pulse started a gallop that she fought to control.

When Travis nudged Midnight into a canter and took off toward the stables, she sat in the saddle for a moment, staring at his retreating form.

For the first time someone was giving her a chance to prove she could do the job. And it didn't hurt that he was smiling at the time.

AJ urged Ace forward, her spirit soaring as the wind whipped past. Travis Maxwell held her future in his hands. She'd have to be very careful he didn't hold her heart, as well.

Chapter Two

Travis slammed through the bunkhouse and stood at the foot of Rusty's bed. He jerked back slightly at the pungent odor that rose up to greet him. The place smelled like dirty socks and leftover pizza.

The linens had been pulled and sat in a pile on the floor. There was nothing to indicate whether or not Rusty had slept there last night or why he hadn't bothered to show up for work today.

Dutch was gone for the weekend, so he'd get no help there. He pulled out his cell and once again punch-dialed Rusty's number, with no results.

"Way to make me look good in front of my new assistant foreman, pal," Travis muttered. He pushed through the back door and got back in the Ute.

"Do I smell funny?" he asked AJ.

"Excuse me?"

"That place looked and smelled worse than a

locker room. Just want to make sure it didn't follow me."

She leaned close and gave a wary sniff. When she did, the scent of chocolate tickled his nose.

"You smell like chocolate."

AJ's eyes widened and she scooted away from him. "I thought this was about you," she said.

"It is. That was just an observation."

"You're fine," AJ murmured.

"Good." He shoved the keys in the ignition, annoyed that his mouth had taken off before his good sense realized what he was doing.

"Cocoa butter," AJ murmured.

Travis's ears perked as he tried to catch her words. "What?"

"It's cocoa butter. You know. Cream." Though she turned away, he glimpsed the pink of embarrassment that touched her face.

"Ah, yeah. Right." Travis put the Ute in gear while silently blaming Rusty for everything and anything, including the awkward exchange with his assistant foreman.

"I take it he wasn't there?" AJ asked.

"No. Maybe we passed him. Let's double back around and check the stables."

Travis did a visual sweep of the stalls as AJ followed. A light was on in the office of the equestrian center manager. Though Travis rapped his knuckles on the glass, Tripp was not fazed. He took his good old time lifting his gaze from the laptop in front of him to acknowledge Travis's presence before waving him into the office.

"Hey, Tripp, do you—"

"Nope." Tripp returned his attention back on the screen.

"What do you mean 'nope'? You don't even know what the question is."

"Rusty."

Travis shook his head. "No pick-up from his cell. I've checked every hidey-hole on this ranch. If he's not dead or near dead, he's going to wish he was."

Tripp shook his head. "You shouldn't have hired him."

"Talking to Lucy, huh?"

"Saw that one coming all by myself."

"Great. By the way, this is the new assistant foreman." He nodded in AJ's direction. "AJ Rowe, meet Tripp Walker."

Tripp slowly unfolded his lanky frame and got to his feet. The man stood at least six-five and carried a scar down the left side of his face.

"Pleased to meet you, ma'am," Tripp said.

"I, uh, thank you," AJ murmured.

"She'll need a horse," Travis said.

A slight nod was the only indication that the stable manager had heard the request. He looked to AJ. "Ace okay?"

"Yes. Absolutely."

He nodded again.

"Thank you."

"We're going to head over to the girls' ranch. Can you find someone to untack our horses?" Travis asked.

"Yep."

"Thanks," Travis said. He cocked his head and AJ followed him out of the stables.

"Quiet, isn't he?"

"They call him the horse whisperer."

"What happened to his…? The scar?"

"Doesn't talk about that, or much of anything."

As they headed back to the Ute, Lucy appeared from around the corner. He recognized the fire in his sister's eyes and the determination in her stride.

This couldn't be good.

"Good morning, AJ," Lucy said with a smile that didn't include him. "Great to have you with us."

"Thanks, Lucy."

"What are you doing here on a Saturday?" Travis asked.

"My kids have riding lessons." Again she directed her conversation to AJ. Finally she turned to him. "We need to talk."

"Whatever you have to say to me, you can say in front of my right-hand man—er, woman."

"Fine. I just received a phone call from the esteemed police chief of Timber."

"Aw, that's nothing. In fact, it's my fault. Sorry. I should have told you. I promised him a discount for renting the retreat center for the law enforcement ball this year."

Lucy crossed her arms. "No, Travis. He was not calling about the ball. It was a courtesy call to inform me that one of our employees is sitting in his jail."

"What?" Travis was all ears as he pulled the Ute keys from his pocket. "What did he do?"

"You know who I'm referring to?"

"I can make an educated guess since I can't find Rusty. What's the charge?"

"Disorderly conduct. Disturbing the peace."

"I've known Rusty for years. Never saw him take a drink, ever."

"Oh, he wasn't drinking. He was, however, dumped by the love of his life. While I feel for the man, this is not the example of leadership and problem-solving skills we want our children to emulate. Plus, we have donors who will hear about his behavior. Rusty is putting everything we've worked hard for these last five years at risk."

Travis took a deep breath at the I-told-you-so that laced his sister's voice.

"Chief Daniels says he's been singing mournful country-western songs since 5:00 a.m. The man is tone deaf and it's driving everyone crazy. He'd like us to bail Rusty out immediately."

"We've got this covered," he assured Lucy. "As I have turned over fire extinguishing, along with the management of the ranch hands, to her, AJ will be letting Rusty go."

He looked to his assistant foreman for confirmation.

AJ pasted a smile on her face and offered a firm nod of confirmation.

Lucy's eyes rounded. "You're good with that, AJ?"

"Absolutely. My job is to make Travis's life easier."

His sister's expression remained doubtful as she looked from AJ to Travis.

"Lucy, we've got this. Trust me," Travis interjected. He put his hands on his sister's shoulders and turned her around. "Go."

"All right, then." Lucy hesitated. "I guess I'll go watch my children ride horses."

"You do that. We have everything under control."

AJ fell into step with him as he moved in the direction of the Ute. "I'm firing Rusty?" she asked.

"Yep. Come on. We'll take my truck."

"Uh, Travis. What exactly did you mean by 'management'? What will I be managing?"

"Everything that concerns the wranglers."

"You're okay with me hiring, too?"

He looked at her. "All part of the job, right?"

"I guess so," she said softly.

"Don't let me regret my decision."

The drive into Timber was quiet. Travis was thankful that AJ kept her focus out the window, eliminating the need for conversation. She was an employee, he reminded himself. Nothing more. No need for chitchat.

When Travis pulled into town, he circled the block, looking for a parking spot.

"Why are there so many cars in town?" AJ asked.

"The Timber Diner."

"I've never in all my life seen this many cars for the diner," she said. "As I recall, their coffee could take paint off a wall."

"New owners. Best food in Timber and it only has a seating capacity of twenty-five. Early bird gets the Denver omelet." When his cell phone rang, he pulled the device from his back pocket and glanced at the screen. Big Heart Ranch again. He nodded to AJ.

"Do you mind if I take this call? I'll catch up."

"No problem."

"I'll drop you off at the station and circle around until I find a parking spot."

When the truck stopped, AJ reached for the door handle.

"Check in with Chief Daniels," he said. "But be warned. He's going to regale you with a story about his latest fishing expedition or his grandchildren. Just nod and smile." He paused. "Oh, and if Rusty gives you any problems—"

AJ placed a hand on his arm and he froze, his mouth wide open as her baby blues met his. "I have this," she said. "Trust me. I have everything under control."

She was tossing his own words right back at him.

Then she opened the passenger door of the truck and hopped down. For a moment he watched her walk down the street, hat in hand. AJ Rowe's mettle was about to be tested. They were both about to find out if Big Heart Ranch's new assistant foreman could do the job she'd been hired to do.

His cell rang again and he put it on speaker phone as he pulled into a parking spot. He put out a few more fires at the ranch before heading to the police station.

The door to the City of Timber police administration building swung open just as Travis placed a hand on the metal push bar. A large man wearing a black Stetson barreled out the door, his shoulder grazing Travis as he stormed past.

"Careful there, friend," Travis said.

The man stopped and turned around, his expression thunderous.

"No. You be careful, Maxwell. Or I might have to mess up that pretty face of yours."

Travis nearly groaned aloud. The man that stood facing him down was none other than Jace McAlester. What the cowboy lacked in height he made up for in bulk. McAlester was as huge as a double-wide and as intimidating as an angry bull just out of the chute.

He stomped through each day with a permanent attitude problem, along with a grudge against Travis that dated back to their professional rodeo days. No telling what had set him off today.

"Good to see you, too, Jace."

"Only good thing about seeing you, Maxwell, is another opportunity to wipe that smile off your face."

"Not today, buddy." Travis raised his hands.

"I am not your buddy."

"That's too bad. No reason old competitors can't be friends."

"In your dreams. I hear your kiddie farm is up against us big boys for that government grant." McAlester sneered.

"That grant is for emerging ranchers."

"The McAlester Ranch deed was turned over to me when my father retired last summer. That means I qualify as manager and foreman of my new ranch."

"That so? Good for you. As I recall, you and I always favored a bit of competition."

"Only when I win, and you can be sure I will. McAlester Ranch is certain to take that grant."

"It's not over until the fat cow sings." Travis chuckled, unable to resist a parting shot for the uptight cowboy.

"What did you call me?" McAlester raged as the ham-hock-size hands he held at his side curled into fists.

"It's an expression, Jace." Travis released a weary sigh. Lucy was going to be very unhappy if he got into a tussle, especially with this sorry excuse for a cowboy. He'd be no better than Rusty, setting a poor example for the kids of Big Heart Ranch.

So instead of drawing his fists, Travis braced himself as Jace pulled back his arm, ready to strike.

"Jace, stop!"

AJ pushed out the door of the police station with Rusty behind her. She jumped between Travis and Jace.

"What are you doing here?" Jace cocked his head, confusion all over his face.

"None of your business," AJ said. "But if you

don't stand down and keep moving, I'm going to get Chief Daniels and then I'm calling Lem."

"You're defending this guy?" Jace asked. He rubbed his fist into the palm of his other hand, eyes wide with annoyance, steam practically rolling from the space between his ears.

"Mr. Maxwell is my boss."

Jace's eyes rounded. "You've got to be kidding me. Does Lem know?"

"I don't report to Lem these days, but yes, he does know I'm back in Timber and working for Big Heart Ranch."

"What about Gus?"

"I'll come and get Gus when I'm able. Lem says he can stay."

"Lem's not in charge. I am, and Gus's keep isn't cheap."

"I'll pay you as soon as I can."

Jace stared at her for a long moment and then shook his head. "So you're telling me that you chose Maxwell over your own family? Over your future?"

She winced at the verbal jab, which opened a truckload of questions in Travis's mind.

"We aren't family, Jace, and you took my future years ago."

At the words, Jace's jaw tightened and he narrowed his eyes. "You think Maxwell has anything to offer but a temporary wrangler position? Wake up, Amanda Jane. No rancher with any sense is going to let a woman run his ranch. Your daddy did you no favors letting you believe that fairy tale."

"The only mistake my daddy ever made was telling me that all cowboys are honorable men."

The silence stretched as everyone froze.

Though AJ had paled, she stood her ground, her gaze unwavering as she looked at the big man.

Jace released a breath, his eyes steely with fury. "You're going to regret siding with Maxwell." The words were low and ice-cold. "Mark my words. He's going down and you're going to go down with him."

"Easy there, McAlester," Travis said as he gently moved AJ aside. "Those are pretty strong threats you're tossing around."

Jace McAlester looked him up and down, contempt all over his face, before he stalked off.

"You okay?" he asked AJ.

She offered a shaky nod and wrapped her arms around herself.

Travis glanced up and down the street, where several people had stopped to see what was going on. He had a hundred questions for his new assistant foreman, but he wasn't going to ask them in the middle of the sidewalk in downtown Timber, Oklahoma.

Instead he turned to Rusty, who sported a black

eye and a split lip. The man's red hair stood on end and his wrinkled, pearl-buttoned, white Western shirt was buttoned all wrong. Drops of blood spattered the once pristine shirt and his Stetson was dusty.

Rusty's eyes were wide and his mouth open as he stared at AJ.

Travis shook his head. "So, Rusty, I see you've met the new assistant foreman."

"Uh, yeah." He blinked and turned to AJ. "She bailed me out."

"What do you have to say for yourself?" Travis asked.

Rusty bowed his head. "I let you down, and I apologize."

Travis turned to AJ. "Did you—"

"She fired me." Rusty looked at AJ and wiped his eyes. "You were right, ma'am. I've got to get my act together. I'm going to look into that counseling. I appreciate your concern."

Travis's eyes popped wide open when Rusty folded him into a bear hug. "Thanks for putting up with me for so long."

"Ah, yeah. Sure, buddy." He stepped back, far from Rusty's reach. "No problem. You understand we're between a rock and a hard place here?"

"Oh, yeah. Absolutely. AJ explained that I was endangering the ranch and the kids."

"She did?"

"Yes, sir."

"Stop by the office on Monday and you can pick up your last check and your personal stuff."

"I'll do that."

"Uh, Rusty, I'll need your keys and your gate security badge."

Rusty dug into the pockets of his baggy Wranglers and pulled them out along with a pair of pliers, a barbed wire stretcher–cable puller and a roll of electrical tape. "Here you go."

Travis blinked at the sight. "How did you get all that in your pockets?"

"I don't know. I was fixing fences when my girlfriend called yesterday. I shoved everything in my pockets and headed to town." He shrugged and turned to leave. "Thanks again."

"Ah, yeah." Travis stared in stunned silence as Rusty moved down the sidewalk. When the wrangler was out of earshot, he turned to AJ. "Nice job."

"Thanks." She cleared her throat. "So I passed the test?"

"First one," he said without meeting her gaze.

"Mind if I ask how you know Jace?" she asked.

"Rodeo. Seems like a long time ago." He cocked his head in question. "What's going on between you two?"

"Going on? Nothing. Jace McAlester is my stepbrother."

Travis blinked, digesting the words. "I did not see that one coming," he murmured. "Jace McAlester is your…"

She nodded.

He shook his head. His new assistant foreman was kin to the man who considered Travis his arch enemy. Oh, yeah. This day just kept getting better.

"Where are you going?" AJ asked as she double-timed her steps to keep up with Travis. She dodged people and pots of geraniums, trying to keep up with the man's long strides down Cedar Avenue and around the corner to Main.

"Back to the ranch. I had to park around down by the library."

Suddenly he stopped and she rammed right into him. "Oomph."

Travis turned and grabbed her arm, steadying her. "You okay?"

Dazed, AJ met his dark eyes and nodded. Yes, she'd be fine once her heart slowed down and breathing commenced. "Why did you stop?"

He pointed to the sign in the office window of the *Timber Independence* on Main Street. "Timber Rodeo. We can sign up here at the newspaper office."

"'We'?"

"One of the things the grant committee looks at is our community involvement."

"You run a ranch for kids. Isn't that overkill?"

"That's our job. They want extra stuff, like volunteering for activities that support the citizens of Timber and participating in local events."

"Are you and your sisters signing up?"

"Guess you hadn't heard. Lucy's pregnant."

"Oh, that's wonderful," AJ said.

"Sure it is. But no rodeo for her. The really exciting news is that she'll have four kids soon. My sister will be too busy with kids to mess with me." He smiled.

"And Emma?"

"Her twin babies are almost two. They're into everything. She's doing well to maintain her sanity." He reviewed the ad on the window listing the categories. "We'll sign you up for barrel racing."

AJ held up a hand. "Whoa, stop right there. I don't have a barrel racing horse."

"Emma does."

"You can't volunteer your sister's horse."

"Sure I can. Besides, she'll be thrilled." He gestured toward the door. "Come on. Let's sign up."

AJ moved back two steps. "I don't have the entry fee on me."

"Big Heart Ranch will sponsor you."

Her mind began a frantic scramble for a way out of the situation. There was no way she was going to volunteer to make a fool of herself in public and in front of her new boss, too.

"Look, Travis," she said, her voice low as she glanced up and down the sidewalk. "I haven't raced since college."

"Relax. The grant aside, the rodeo is for charity. The idea is to make a showing for the ranch."

Travis pulled open the door to the newspaper office. "Hey, there." He offered a greeting to the young clerk at the reception desk.

Her eyes rounded and she released a small gasp of surprise. "It's you."

Travis glanced around, praying she was talking to someone else. "Me?"

"You're the guy on the cover of *Tulsa Now*." The perky brunette reached for the magazine on the corner of her desk.

"You're new." He frowned with obvious annoyance.

"Yes. Avery Barnes, aspiring journalist. I'm an intern here for the semester."

"Travis Maxwell and this is AJ Rowe."

AJ smiled, but the young woman had eyes only for Travis. AJ could have walked in tarred and feathered and Avery Barnes, aspiring journalist, wouldn't have noticed.

"Sooner or Cowboy?" Travis asked.

"Neither. University of Tulsa. May I have your autograph?"

"I guess so." The words rode on a long-suffering sigh.

She handed him a marker and he scrawled his name on the cover of the magazine.

"Thank you so much, Mr. Maxwell," Avery gushed.

"Now, may I please have a couple of applications to the Timber Rodeo?"

"You're participating?" Her eyes lit up.

"Yeah. So is my assistant foreman here."

"There are some really nice sponsor prizes this year," she said as she collected the paperwork.

"We're here to support the event. If we win, we'll donate the funds back to the community."

"May I quote you?" Avery asked.

"This isn't an interview."

"It could be." Her eyes rounded with hope. "The paper hasn't gone to press this week yet. This would look great on the front page with your picture."

"The ranch director could help you out with that. In fact, she could give you a tour of the ranch. That would make for a nice feature article."

"But you're the Bachelor of the Year."

"That's old news," Travis said.

"But—"

"Here's my card. That's the ranch number on there. Call and ask for Lucy Maxwell Harris." He glanced around. "The paperwork for the rodeo?"

"Right here." She handed him two packets. "Turn everything back in by the end of the week."

"Will do. Thank you."

AJ followed him out the door.

"Was it just me or was that girl plain irritating?" he asked AJ.

"She was crushing on you."

Travis groaned. "I blame Lucy," he said as he strode toward the truck.

"How is that Lucy's fault?"

"Trust me, it is, but, generally, even if it isn't her fault I blame Lucy. That's how it works. You blame your big sister."

"I don't have a big sister," she murmured.

"Brother?"

AJ shook her head.

"You're the oldest?"

"I'm an only child."

"Well, I'm sorry to hear that. My sisters do come in handy at times." He grinned.

Travis got in and closed his door. He stared at the newspaper office and shook his head. "That just rubs me raw."

"That I don't have siblings?"

"No. I'm talking about the clerk in the newspaper office. You know, the way some folks act like it's all about the package. What's on the outside and not on the inside. Judge me by my merit, not my face on some magazine." He paused and turned toward her. "Know what I mean?"

AJ met his gaze without blinking. *You have no*

idea, cowboy. The words nearly escaped before she bit them back. "I think I might," she said instead.

Travis stared for a moment before his eyes widened. Then he lowered his head and focused on putting the key in the ignition. "Yeah. I guess you do," he murmured.

Silence filled the cab as he backed up and headed back to the ranch.

"Did I mention that you did a nice job with Rusty?" Travis said minutes later.

"Pardon me?" She turned to look at him.

"Rusty. Nice job. Did I say that?"

"Yes, you did. Thank you."

They drove in awkward silence until Travis glanced over at her, a question on his face.

"What is it?" she finally asked.

"You're an only child and Lemuel McAlester is your stepfather?"

"Yes. When I was in college, my mother married Lem and they renamed my father's ranch. Lem is a good man, but he never really knew what to do with a grown stepdaughter. He takes care of Gus for me and I try to stop by or call when I can. Not as often once Jace left the rodeo circuit and moved to the ranch."

"Lem turned the spread over to Jace?"

She nodded. "Jace is his only child. Our parents married after we both had left home. Me for college and Jace for the rodeo circuit."

Travis shook his head. "Bet that was a surprise. Finding out Jace was your family."

"It wasn't so bad when my mother was alive. She provided a buffer. Once I lost her, my entire world was turned upside down. Jace made it clear everything would be his when Lem retired, so I never looked back."

"I'm sorry, AJ." His dark eyes were warm with concern.

"Thank you," she murmured.

"I don't understand why Lem didn't step in. After all, that ranch was yours, as well."

"My stepfather is no different than most of the old-timers in Oklahoma. He believes a woman's place is in the kitchen." She shook her head. "He forgets that, besides cooking, I can also mend fences, rope and brand cattle."

Travis offered a solemn nod. "How long ago since you left?"

"Nearly ten years, though it turned out the joke was on Jace. His father didn't trust him enough to retire until this year."

Travis rolled down the window. "You mind?"

"Not at all."

His fingers tapped out a beat on the steering wheel in time to the country-western song on the radio.

"Funny our paths haven't crossed before now," he finally said.

"How long have you been in Timber?"

"A little over five years."

"How did you end up here with the ranch?" AJ asked.

"After we were fished out of foster care, by a cousin of our mother's, we lived in Pawhuska. My sisters and I didn't even know about the land in Timber until she passed on and left it to us."

AJ nodded and watched the tall prairie grass out the truck window.

"So what's your plan?" Travis asked.

"My plan?" She looked at him.

"Yeah. I'm guessing you aren't here for the long haul."

"What's that supposed to mean?"

"Big Heart Ranch obviously is not the last stop on your trail."

AJ stared at him, suddenly bone-weary. If only he knew how much she longed to be in it for the long haul, as he put it. She took a deep breath, shoving back the emotion burning behind her eyes. The emotion she could never reveal because every time she did, she was disappointed. Again.

"I'll stop when I know that I'm where God wants me to be. Then it will be time to put down roots."

"What's if that's Big Heart Ranch?"

"I'm not ruling it out."

Silence hung in the air as AJ considered his words. Her plan? God's plan? She'd take either at the moment, praying one of those plans included an end to her drifting, and finding a place where she was actually wanted. Needed.

"Mind if I ask a personal question?" he finally said.

"I won't know if I mind until you ask."

"Fair enough." A small smile lifted his lips. "Who's Gus?"

"My horse. A gift from my mother."

"Why don't you move him over to Big Heart?"

"It's complicated."

"I understand complicated. Why don't you try me?"

"Look, I'd rather not move Gus and have to move him back if this job doesn't work out. Besides, Gus had a pretty big vet bill a while back and I'm still paying Lem for that."

"This is your call, but I'm happy to help."

"I'd rather do things my way."

"Understood." Travis cleared his throat. "Any idea how Jace knows that we're applying for the grant?"

"What?" Her head jerked up at the quietly spoken question and she met Travis's gaze.

"How does—"

"I have no idea." She paused, struggling to read

between the lines of his question. "You don't think I told him, do you?"

"Just asking." Travis took a deep breath.

"'Just asking' sounds an awful lot like an accusation to me."

"Whoa." He raised a hand. "I'm just doing the math."

"You can subtract me from your equation."

"I apologize," Travis said.

AJ was silent, uncertain if he was sincere.

"Look," Travis said. "You don't know me and I really don't know you. All I'm doing is trying to figure things out."

Trying to figure things out. She turned to look out the window without answering. What was there to figure out? In truth, she and Travis were alike in many ways. Maybe too many ways. The thought was far from comforting and it wouldn't secure her position at Big Heart Ranch. Not if her boss didn't trust her.

"We sure have our work cut out for us," Travis mused aloud minutes later. "Take tomorrow off to study the grant material. On Monday we hit the ground running. You'll go to Tulsa with me to look at starter calves. There's a special sale going on at an auction house near Sapulpa and then we can pick up the supplies I ordered in Pawhuska on the way back."

"What about hiring? And who will do Rusty's work in the meantime?"

"I have confidence you'll figure it out. That's what days off are for."

"You just said—"

"Welcome to my world. You'll be juggling saddles from this point on. And remember, that grant is my number-one priority. We're competing against Jace McAlester and he's going to do everything he can to see that he wins."

Juggling saddles she could handle, but why did she feel like she was caught in the middle of a tornado and the chance she'd make it out untouched was slim to nothing? She was a woman of her word, though, and was willing to pledge her heart and soul to Big Heart Ranch for the next ninety days with the hope she wouldn't regret the decision. Once the grant was behind them, she'd reevaluate her position on the ranch. That was unless she didn't last ninety days.

Chapter Three

AJ stood on the porch of the bunkhouse, looking out at the ranch while sipping a cup of coffee. Dark clouds covered the sky, shrouding everything in black and gray, even as the sun struggled to wake the land at 6:30 a.m. The month of April brought the heaviest amounts of precipitation to this part of Oklahoma. Today was about to give evidence to that.

Her first Sunday at Big Heart Ranch. Despite the weather, there was a peace to the land that reminded her of days on Red River Ranch, her daddy's spread. What would her life be like if her parents hadn't died? AJ pushed the thought aside.

The only thing she carried from the past was the promise she'd made to herself when she'd buried her mother. Someday she'd be a permanent part of a ranch that needed her. Wanted her. And she intended to keep that promise.

Something moved to her left and AJ switched on the porch light. A roadrunner dashed across the yard, his long, slender legs kicking up red dust.

Sunrise would arrive within the hour. Her plan was to be well on her way to checking the fences by then. She'd be done and could shower and catch the late service at the Timber Community Church if all went well.

Stepping back into the bunkhouse she rinsed out her cup and tidied up, leaving everything the way she'd found it. Nothing out of place. Rue Butterfield had left last night and now AJ had the bunkhouse to herself. She remained unsettled and a bit afraid to hope that she might have a future here. Lucy and Emma Maxwell were her biggest supporters. Now all she had to do was to continue to prove to Travis she could do the job.

Rue's King James Bible was still on her bed and AJ peeked at the open page as she walked by. A verse had been underlined with a red pen. Proverbs 3:5-6. "Trust in the LORD with all thine heart; and lean not unto thine own understanding. In all thy ways acknowledge Him, and He shall direct thy paths."

AJ put a hand to her heart and swallowed. That was pretty much the story of her life. She said a silent prayer as she tucked a disposable rain slicker into the pocket of her denim jacket, grabbed her hat and carefully closed the bunkhouse door behind her.

The air was ripe with the scent of rain and, despite her prayer, an undefinable dread followed her as she headed to the Ute. Shivers danced down her arms all the way to the equestrian center. Why the ominous feeling? She'd checked spread fences dozens of times before. She could do this job.

AJ parked the Ute and hurried her steps. The stable door creaked with the effort of sliding open the latch to reveal the glowing amber of floor track lights.

Her hand searched the wall, finally locating the switches and turning on half the overhead lights. She walked down to Ace's stall and called a soft greeting.

The horse nickered in acknowledgment. AJ dug in her pocket for the apple she'd brought and pulled out her pocketknife to cut it. She smiled as Ace inched closer, sniffing and snorting with anticipation.

This was the same routine she and Gus had each day.

She missed her horse. Gus was a gift from her mother. The blue roan ranch horse wasn't getting younger, either. Lem had promised her he'd look after Gus when she'd left, and she prayed he'd kept that promise. Mostly she tried not to think about the situation, because if she did she'd get all teary-eyed. There was no room in her life for sentiment.

Once Ace finished chomping the apple, AJ grabbed a brush from the tack room and found her saddle and a blanket. She entered the stall and gave Ace a gentle nose-rub before brushing the animal's coat and examining her legs.

"Morning, AJ."

AJ jumped at Travis's voice and the brush tumbled from her hand to the ground.

"Sorry," he said.

"I was thinking, and didn't hear you," AJ murmured. Picking up the brush, she faced him. As usual Travis's eyes did the talking. Today they spoke of his surprise at seeing her in the stables this early and maybe a hint of respect.

She turned back to Ace and, for moments, the only sound was the rhythmic strokes of the brush, along with horse's nickering.

AJ focused on the job at hand, trying to block out the man. The rapid tripping of her heart when he was near confused her. Once again her mind scrambled to understand. Why this man? Why now? In her line of work she couldn't afford romantic notions about cowboys she worked with.

Bitter memories crowded in. Hadn't she learned anything at her last position? The range boss had taken a liking to her and though she'd kept him at a distance, rumors had persisted. Enough so that the other ranch hands had made her life impossible. She'd been forced to walk away after giving that spread two years of her life.

It took all her concentration to tack up Ace while Travis stood by with his arms looped over the top of the stall.

Settling the blanket on Ace's back, she hefted the saddle into position before turning to Travis again. "Are you planning to observe for the duration?"

"I'm trying to figure you out. I thought I told you to take the day off. It's Sunday. I'll be in big trouble if my sisters think I kept you from church."

"You juggle saddles, too, as I recall." She smiled. "And I plan to attend the late service."

"I'm going to have to watch my words. This is the second time I've had them dangled in my face."

AJ adjusted the cinch, tucking her head away so as not to laugh.

"You're going to check fences, aren't you?"

"I am." She nodded. "I looked at the schedule. Rusty was on for this morning. I'm his supervisor, so it's my responsibility."

"Two days in and you've exceeded expectations. I'll give you points for that alone."

She met his gaze, unable to hide her surprise. "Is that a compliment?"

Travis shrugged. "I guess it is."

"Maybe you should have raised your expectations before now."

His lips curved into a begrudging smile. "Maybe."

AJ opened the stall and led Ace to the center of the stable.

"I'll meet you outside," Travis said.

"You're joining us?"

"Don't want my new assistant foreman to get lost out there."

"I'm actually very good with directions."

"I haven't given you any directions."

"You said to check the fences."

"Good to have company the first time," he said as he headed to Midnight's stall.

AJ shook her head. Was the man determined to be contrary? The odd thing was that she'd never once had company doing anything on any other ranch. No, everyone had steered clear of her, careful not to divide their allegiance, because they all knew she was only a place-holder. They were happy to spread rumors but silent when it came to admitting she was always one of the hardest-working ranch hands on duty.

Now she had a handsome cowboy following her around and, while any other woman would be glad, it raised red flags for AJ. Travis Maxwell was the boss. Her father had taught her long ago that fraternizing with someone you worked with was like walking through a minefield.

The simple truth was, the job aside, she hadn't found a man she could trust since her father died. She'd trusted her last boss and he'd failed to defend her when the rumors swirled.

The only long-term relationship in her life was Gus. Gus never lied and never let her down.

Spits of rain landed on her as she settled into the saddle. AJ shifted and picked up the reins, urging Ace forward. She didn't have all day and, by the looks of things, the sky was getting ready to burst wide open. Travis would have to catch up.

And he did. Minutes later the thunder of hooves indicated Travis and Midnight were at her side.

"What? You couldn't wait?"

Annoyance marred his face and AJ struggled not to laugh. Travis Maxwell did not like to be bested.

"The clocking is ticking. It's about to pour and I still haven't made it to see that cattle of yours."

"Northwest pasture. See that big oak tree out there?"

"Yes."

"That's your landmark. Veer right."

It took her a moment to realize why he was giving her directions. By then he and Midnight were racing toward the tree, leaving her and Ace literally in the dust.

"That was a false start if ever there was one," she called after him.

Travis's laughter rode on the wind, only encouraging AJ to lean forward in the saddle and spur Ace into the gray dawn. Rounding the massive oak tree, she closed the gap between them. Straight ahead in the distance, on a small grassy knoll, the silhouette of the cattle came into view.

"You're not too bad in the saddle," he observed when she caught up. His face was without expression as he narrowed his eyes in assessment.

"I told you in the interview. I was raised on a horse."

"People say a lot of things in interviews. Ask Rusty."

AJ jerked back slightly at the comment and pinned him with her gaze, but he had tipped his hat back to look at the sky.

"Uh-oh," Travis murmured. "Here it comes."

He was right. Fat drops turned into sheets of rain in a heartbeat. AJ pulled the folded square of clear slicker from her pocket, shook it out and slipped the plastic over her head.

"Got another one of those in your pocket?"

"No. Sorry. I didn't think—"

"That's okay. I won't melt, but just to be sure, let's duck under the oak tree. That canopy will help some."

She turned Ace around and followed Travis

beneath the stretching arms of the massive tree. For moments they sat in silence as water fell in constant beats onto the hard red clay. The greedy ground drank until full, then the water began to overflow, running downhill in winding rivulets around the horses' hooves and over the roots of the oak.

Her father called sudden downpours like this "toad stranglers."

"What's that sound?" Travis asked moments later. He inched Midnight forward and peered through the curtain of rain.

"Thunder?"

"No. Sounds like a truck bouncing over the ground." He continued to search the landscape. "But there's no road out here."

"Travis, look. Over there. You're right. It is a truck, coming up on the other side of your steers from the woods."

"Sure is. A truck and a trailer." He released a breath. "Cattle rustlers. Must have cut the fence and come around the lodge."

"You have fifteen head. Why would anyone take a risk for so few cattle?"

"They're worth a bit over a thousand dollars each at market, that's why." He pulled up the collar of his jacket and lifted the reins. "Whoever those rustlers are, they surely know we're easy pickings out here."

"Are your calves tagged or hot branded?"

"Tagged. And, yeah, I know that doesn't stop rustlers. They remove the tag. I was hoping we wouldn't have to hot brand."

"No cameras out here?"

"Cameras are in the budget for this year. Add that to your list."

"My list?"

"Yeah, of all the things I've let slide because I haven't had reliable help."

"What are we going to do right now?"

Travis pushed his hat low on his ears. "The only thing we can do. Save the stock."

"What if they're armed?"

"I can't let them walk onto our land and take my cattle, can I?"

"You can call the Timber police."

"Chief Daniels and his two-man police posse? Seriously? It's Sunday. If I call now, I'll get dispatch and she'll tell me that they'll be out here to take a report later." He shook his head. "No one is going to miss church for my little herd. If I want to save the cattle program that we haven't even launched yet, I have to act."

Overhead the clouds crashed, punctuating his words. The sound was followed by a crooked fork of yellow and pink light that flashed across the sky, illuminating everything for a brief moment.

Midnight balked at the sound and Ace reared up, side-stepping in distress.

"Easy, Ace," AJ crooned, doing her best to soothe the animal.

"Can it get any better than this?" Travis muttered. "We're under a tree, in a lightning storm, while my cattle are being stolen."

Once again, thunder was chased by a shock of electricity that split the sky. Ace kicked her hind legs, offering a loud, agitated whinny before she bucked and took off.

"Whoa!" AJ reached for the saddle horn, holding tight and fighting for control as the mare stampeded in a path straight toward the rustlers.

One more crash of noise had Ace spinning around and changing direction in a mad frenzy. AJ slid helplessly to the ground and landed with a thud and a splash right in a puddle.

"AJ," Travis yelled, concern lacing his voice. He jumped from Midnight and was by her side in an instant.

Disgusted, AJ waved a muddy hand in gesture. "I'm fine. I slid and landed on my backside. Go get your rustlers."

Travis laughed. "You scared them away. They backed up, circled around and disappeared through the trees and out the same way they got in."

"Did you get a look at the truck pulling that trailer?" she asked.

"Dark-colored pickup, maybe black or brown."

"Or burgundy?"

"Hard to tell. Raining too hard." The sky flickered with lightning as she spoke.

"Was it a Ford?"

"I told you it was raining too hard. The only thing I know for certain is that the truck is covered in mud." He swiped at the water on his face and looked at her. "You recognize the vehicle?"

AJ hesitated. Was it Jace's burgundy pickup truck? Surely her stepbrother wasn't that reckless. She couldn't be sure and she wasn't going to point the finger without more proof.

"It's raining too hard to be sure," AJ answered. She positioned her palms on the ground and tried to gain traction; instead she slipped on the slick mud.

Travis put his arm around her. "Let me help you."

"I've got it." She moved from his touch, struggling to a standing position. "Where's Ace?"

"That horse is way smarter than we are. She'll be back at the stables before we arrive, I imagine."

"How am I going to get back?"

"You'll have to ride with me."

"No way. I'm covered with mud." She eyed him. And no way was she sharing a saddle with Travis. Her peace of mind couldn't handle being that close to the man.

Scooping up the stallion's reins with one hand and the saddle horn with the other, Travis mounted Midnight. Reaching down to AJ, he held out a hand. "Come on. We'll grab the Ute and fix that fence. Then we're going to have to move the cattle closer to the barn until I can get someone to work night shift."

"You don't have enough wranglers to work day shift."

"Thanks for pointing out the obvious."

"Aren't you at least going to report this when we get back?"

"I'm not calling Chief Daniels out to the ranch on a Sunday to tell him that we almost got rustled and that we can't identify the vehicle much less the thieves."

"You're embarrassed?"

"Yeah, I am. I'll stop by and file a report on Monday." He glanced at the sky. "Looks like most of the fireworks in the sky have died down." Again he offered a hand.

"I'll walk."

"I'm not going to argue with you while water drips down my back. Let's go."

"Fine." AJ took his hand and let him hoist her up into the saddle. She sat stiffly as he reached around her for the reins.

"Are you comfortable?" Travis asked.

"Absolutely not," she murmured.

Travis burst out laughing. "Relax," he said close to her ear.

Relax? Not likely when she was a hairbreadth away from Travis Maxwell. Day two on the job and she'd lost her horse, was covered in mud and sitting in the saddle with her boss, smack dab in the middle of a pasture waiting for lightning to strike them.

He shall direct thy paths.

The verse danced through her head as Travis Maxwell directed the stallion back to the stables.

AJ gently pulled up the reins on Gus and moved closer to the top of the McAlester Ranch pasture. It had been a long day.

Once she and Travis had finished with the cattle, she'd gotten cleaned up and headed to church. Barely sneaking in the doors on time, she'd spied Travis across the crowded chapel and he'd offered a nod as he sat with his sisters and their families. She'd tried to resist but was unable to stop peeking at the Maxwells.

It had been a very long time since she'd sat in a church pew with family. AJ pushed away the gut-clenching sadness and instead focused on the prairie grassland before her that stretched as far as she could see.

She had too many things to be thankful for and that was what she needed to remember.

The sun finally poked through the clouds and began to warm her as she sat in the saddle. AJ took a deep breath and inhaled the sweet earthy scent that came after a good downpour.

A pounding of hooves had her looking south. She rubbed her eyes and blinked at the sight of a horse and rider approaching. Surely she was hallucinating. Travis Maxwell was riding her stepfather's horse and headed in her direction.

"Just passing through?" she asked when he got closer.

"You might say that." He grinned and pushed his hat to the back of his head. "You'd be wrong, but you might say that."

She stared pointedly at the horse he rode. "You know, they still hang horse thieves."

Laughter spilled from his lips and lit up his face. The effect left her a tangle of emotions, forcing her to avert her gaze.

"I am many things, but a horse thief is not on the list. Your stepfather told me to take this pretty paint." Travis patted the gelding's neck. "In fact, he practically begged me to. The man seemed impressed to meet me. And he never even mentioned *Tulsa Now* magazine."

Her eyes widened. "Lem McAlester made you take his favorite horse?"

"Yeah." He grinned. "'Course it didn't hurt to find out that Lem and my mother's cousin knew each other. He had some nice words to say about my family."

AJ offered a harrumph.

"You know, AJ, this may come as a surprise, but lots of folks like me. Why is that so hard to believe?"

"What's hard to believe is that you had the guts to come out here knowing Jace is gunning for you."

"Oh, I knew your stepbrother wasn't here."

"How did you know that?"

"I saw him in Timber, walking into the diner with one of his cronies. When I wasn't looking, my own truck detoured here on the way home. I saw your pickup and stopped."

"Why?" she asked.

"I had a hunch." His expression became serious and his gaze locked with hers. "And I think you did, too."

"We can't prove it was Jace this morning," she murmured.

"Why did you come, then?"

"Same as you. I wanted to get a look at his pickup, but I missed him." She released a frustrated breath. "Do you think it was him?"

"Doesn't matter what I think. As you said, we can't prove a thing. The only thing I'm sure of is that he won't get a second chance to mess with my cattle."

"I'm having a hard time wrapping my head around the fact it could be Jace."

"Then you don't know your stepbrother like you think you do. I've seen him in action more than once. Foolhardy, out of control and spiteful."

"I understand why he's mad at me." She looked at Travis. "Why is he out to get you?"

"Oh, the usual. A bronc and a woman. It was a long time ago."

A woman? AJ tried to process that information. She glanced at his profile, unsettled at the notion that he'd had a woman important enough to fight over.

"Jace is playing a dangerous game of revenge," Travis said with a shake of his head.

"Poor Lem. He has no idea."

"Should you tell him?"

"I can't be the one."

"You might want to rethink that decision." He glanced around. "What are you doing here anyhow?"

"I thought I may as well give my horse a workout while Jace was gone."

"That's Gus, huh?" He nodded toward the blue roan. "Beautiful horse."

AJ smiled and patted the gelding's neck.

"I told you I'll get him out to Big Heart."

"I'm giving that offer some thought. The truth is, I'm not sure you'll keep me employed long enough to make moving a horse a worthwhile proposition."

"Trust is a two-way street, AJ."

"Yes. So I've heard. Heard it when Lem promised my mother that my father's ranch would be mine someday. Heard it when my last boss said I was on the fast track to assistant foreman. Seems like trust works well with horses but not so much with people."

A long silence stretched and AJ dared to peek at the man sitting next to her. She followed his gaze as he turned in the saddle and scanned the lush greenery. Spring wildflowers had turned the fields to a colorful panorama. Bitterweed, sage and Indian grass were already beginning to bloom.

"So this was your spread growing up?" Travis finally asked.

"Yes," she said, her lips curving into a smile. "Red River Ranch."

"Where are the bison grazing?" he asked.

"Seriously?" she scoffed. "Jace is about as open-minded as you are when it comes to sustainability and innovation in ranching."

"Ouch. That hurt."

She didn't answer.

"Looks like those fences could use some attention," he said with a nod to the sagging wire and rotting posts.

"Everything around here could use some attention. This place never looked like this when my daddy was alive or when I was taking care of things." She shook her head. "I probably should come out and help Lem with the fences, instead of riding Gus."

"Maybe Jace should be helping with the fences."

"Not going to happen anytime soon. He's headed to Tulsa for the night. Lem says Jace is going to buy cattle on Monday."

Travis slapped his hand on his thigh. "Which is exactly what you and I are going to do tomorrow. The only difference is my fences are in good shape."

She nodded. Lifting the reins, AJ let Gus take the lead.

"Where are you headed?" Travis asked.

"I promised Gus a ride." She clucked her tongue. The horse complied and picked up speed. A glance over her shoulder told her Travis had, too.

"What's your assessment of Big Heart? I mean so far?" he said when he caught up. "I guess that's not really a fair question. Two days and you've seen nothing but trouble."

"You have a fine operation at Big Heart," she said. "You should be proud."

"Okay, that's the canned answer. What do you really think?"

"That is what I really think."

"Well, I'll call it good once I get this grant and can expand the cattle operation. Then I'll feel like I've pulled my weight."

"Is that what this is all about?" she asked, understanding dawning.

"What do you mean?"

"The whole grant thing. It's bigger than starting a program. This is about you."

He frowned and looked at her. "My ego is nowhere in the mix, if that's what you're saying. But yeah, I'll sleep better when I'm certain I'm contributing my fair share to the ministry of Big Heart."

"Seems to me you already are."

"Nothing is as it seems. I'm running fifteen head. My sister Lucy handles the entire ranch staff and Emma tends to the children of Big Heart. Why, Tripp has more horses to keep track of than I have cattle."

"Aren't you responsible for the other livestock, as well?"

"Yeah, that's me. Travis Maxwell—poultry, swine and goat supervisor."

AJ tried not to smile. He could deny it, but this was all about ego.

"I can't expand the operation without help. That's where you come in." He ran a hand over his face. "All I'm saying is that this project means a lot to me. I'm praying you're going to be on board one hundred percent, because no way can I do it alone. You and I are stuck with each other for the duration."

"I am committed, Travis. At least for ninety days."

"Fair enough." He nodded. "Though commitment is one thing. What I really need is your loyalty."

Confused, she narrowed her eyes. "What do you mean?"

"You're going to have to make a decision." Unflinching, he met her gaze. "It's obvious you're still tied to McAlester Ranch."

"That's not true."

"Sure it is. You're wallowing in regret."

She inhaled sharply as the truth of his words punched her in the gut.

"You have to decide where your loyalties are going to be. Big Heart Ranch or McAlester Ranch?" Travis straightened in the saddle. "Because everything we do from this point on is all about that grant and failure isn't an option."

AJ looked around at the land she loved so much. She bit her lip and fought emotion as she ran a hand over Gus's neck.

Travis was right. Her father's ranch was her past. Nothing she did could change things. The cowboy was asking her to commit to the future and move forward. Could she do that?

In a split second she made the decision, knowing it was the right decision.

She nodded as she met Travis's expectant gaze. "You can count on me. I'm full-in, Travis," she murmured. The words were true. There was a peace in her heart telling her that this was the path the Lord had set her on.

Chapter Four

"Let's head over to the sale barn," Travis said to AJ as they left the auction registration office with their bidding number. "I want to look at the starter calves."

"Have you got the auction itch today?" she asked.

He chuckled. "No. I've made that mistake before. Jumping in and being swept up by the excitement."

AJ offered a grin that said she understood what he was talking about.

"But I will admit that the market's low right now," he continued. "A good day to be a buyer. I'm excited about that, and I'm hoping we can come away with something to smile about."

The huge metal door to the sale barn was open and the pungent odor of hay, cattle and manure invited them to the arena that had been portioned into pens. Unseasonably warm spring weather warranted the use of huge fans to move the thick air. Above them, scaffolding walkways allowed buyers to peer down and evaluate the many lots of animals.

Travis rolled up the sleeves of his denim shirt, adjusted his Stetson and led the way through the maze of pens, checking cattle and taking pictures of lot numbers with his phone. To the uneducated eye, the layout seemed to make no sense, but he'd been evaluating this particular sale house for weeks, walking up and down the rows, crunching the numbers and monitoring prices to prepare for the day he'd bring another load of starter calves home to Big Heart Ranch.

A group of smiling cowgirls walked by, their gazes flirtatious as they inadvertently blocked the path in front of Travis and AJ. Travis grabbed AJ's hand and tugged her past them. "'Scuse us, ladies," he said with a tip of his hat.

"I think they were looking to be your posse," AJ chided.

"I'll pass," he muttered. Travis reluctantly released her hand as they continued to walk by pens, assessing cattle. Holding AJ's hand seemed almost right, and that was a puzzlement.

They continued to walk, viewing cattle and exchanging looks as they went, with no need for words.

"What did you think about that last lot?" AJ finally asked.

"You read my mind. That lot is the top of my list." His phone buzzed and he pulled the cell from his pocket. "Good timing. That's Dutch's text. He's ready to hit the road with the trailer as soon as I call him back with news we got what we came for. We can load out and get home before the auction is over."

"Your senior wrangler is an interesting character," AJ observed as he tucked his phone away.

He smiled. "You mean *your* senior wrangler."

"I guess technically that is correct." She picked up her pace to keep up with his long strides. "He has some crazy idea that his seniority precludes him from getting up before dawn."

"He told you that?"

"Not in so many words. In fact, I can't repeat what he said when I woke him before sunrise this morning."

Travis couldn't hold back a belly laugh. *"You?"* He adjusted his hat. "You woke up Dutch?"

"Yes, I did. And I'll do it every day until we have clarity on the issue."

He stopped walking and stared at her in stunned surprise. "Dutch and his seniority have been an ongoing battle for the last five years."

"The battle is about to end."

"You're a mighty brave woman, AJ Rowe."

"I'm persistent. My father taught me that. I may go down, but I'll go down fighting."

"You can be sure that I'll keep my eye on the situation. If you're successful, a steak dinner is in your future."

"Start saving your pennies. I'm a big eater."

He laughed with pure pleasure at the fire in her blue eyes. Dinner with AJ held an enticing promise, even if it meant facing the wrath of Dutch. "Go for it," he said.

"Since we're going for it, I'm working on the schedule."

"Okay," he prompted.

"I went and introduced myself to your college boys this morning. They tell me you let them have every weekend off."

"They have to study."

AJ frowned as she looked at him. "You're kind of a soft touch, aren't you?"

"You've been talking to Lucy."

"No. Why?"

"That's her mantra." Once more he paused in the aisle. "You may as well hear the truth from me. Each of the Maxwells approaches life differently. Lucy's the bossy one. Takes pleasure in telling people what to do. Emma is the baby and our charmer. She finesses everything and everyone."

"And you?"

He rubbed his chin. "I avoid confrontation at all cost."

"Have you considered therapy?"

Travis chuckled at her flat honesty. "Cowboys don't do therapy. I'm a lover, not a fighter. Nothing wrong with that. Isn't that Biblical? Turn the other cheek. Besides, I pay you to handle the drama."

"True enough." She released a breath. "And I'm not without sympathy. I worked my way through college on ranches. Except, in my book, everyone rotates weekends."

"You're the boss. But if you get knocked off the Christmas card list don't say I didn't warn you."

"Making a few wranglers unhappy is the least of my concerns. We're covering Rusty's job and trying to watch the herd at night. That's stretching everything and everybody thin."

"How about those cameras?" he asked.

"You only just told me about them yesterday."

"Call Lucy and nudge her."

"I'll do that when we finish here."

He started walking again. "We better move. They'll be getting to the calves anytime now."

When a tall, fresh-faced cowboy stepped into Travis's path he was forced to stop short.

Rafe Diego. Just what he didn't need. The young wrangler's hat was pushed to the back of his head and the smirk on his face made it clear that he was up to something.

"Travis Maxwell." The cowboy strutted closer, showing off his oversize brass rodeo buckle and shiny boots. "Haven't seen you with a lady except your lovely sisters since—"

Travis cleared his throat, effectively cutting off the arrogant cowboy. "How is it you're able to talk with those boots tucked in your mouth, Diego?"

Rafe ignored him and immediately turned the full wattage of his smile on AJ. She, in turn, shifted her attention to a pair of Angus yearlings in the pen behind her.

"Something I can help you with?" Travis asked.

"Simply being neighborly."

"Great. See you around, then, neighbor."

"Hold on there," Rafe said with a hand on Travis's arm. "Don't you want to introduce me to your lady friend?"

Travis narrowed his eyes and stared at Diego's hand.

The cowboy wisely stepped back.

With a pained sigh, Travis turned to AJ. "AJ Rowe, this is Rafe Diego."

Rafe tipped his hat. "Please to meet you, ma'am." He cocked his head to one side as though serious thinking might be going on between his ears. "Rowe? Weren't you up in Skiatook at Lake Ranch?"

AJ tensed and put her hands in her pockets. "Yes."

Rafe offered a slow insinuating nod, his gaze going from Travis to AJ.

"Take care," Travis said with a nod to AJ to keep moving. Whatever was going on in the cowboy's head, he didn't like it. "See you later, Rafe. We've got a meeting with some calves."

"Whoa. Not so fast. Timber charity rodeo is coming up. You plan on participating?"

"The ranch will have several representatives."

"Bronc riding?" Rafe asked.

"Could be." Travis narrowed his eyes. "Why?"

"Prize money's looking real good."

"That so? The Timber Rodeo's only two weeks away. Shouldn't you be getting in shape instead of jawing with me?"

Rafe stood straight and sucked in his gut. "I am in shape, old man."

Travis clamped his mouth shut, not willing to engage further with the cowboy. Rafe was the next generation of bronc riders. Recently off the circuit, he was as cocky as he was talented.

Once more, Travis began to move on to the next row of pens, in the direction of the auction ring.

"I heard you lost Rusty," Rafe called.

Travis pushed up his sleeve and examined his watch before he faced the cowboy again. "That was less than twenty-four hours ago. How did you hear about it already?"

"Are you kidding? That's the scuttle of the day at the Timber Diner. Word spreads faster there than honey on a hot biscuit." He grinned. "So, are you hiring?"

"AJ is the assistant foreman at Big Heart Ranch," Travis said. He tilted his head back to take a swig from his water bottle.

"The what?" Rafe's head jerked back with surprise. "You sure do get around. I guess it helps to be a pretty little thing, don't it?"

Travis started coughing at Rafe's words.

"You okay?" AJ asked.

"Yeah. Yeah." The words were choked out. "But he's not going to be."

"I have this," she returned. AJ stepped right up in Rafe's face and looked him up and down. At five-feet-six, she was nose to his chin. That didn't stop her. "I don't care what you heard, Mr. Diego, but I've earned my position wherever I've worked." Distaste was all over her as she spoke. "If you can handle taking orders from a woman, then yes, I'm hiring. Be sure to send your résumé to Big Heart Ranch, attention of the 'pretty little thing.'"

The cowboy's face paled. "Yes, ma'am."

Travis took a perverse pleasure in the dress-down and even more in seeing the cowboy's retreating form.

"Well played," Travis said. He offered his knuckles to her for a fist bump. Eyes still lit with fire, AJ touched her small fist to his. "I should take you with me more often," he murmured.

Her face pinked at the words. "I guess you probably want to know what he was talking about. Lake Ranch, I mean."

"Not really," Travis said. "As you said, you earned the right to do the hiring on Big Heart Ranch. That's all I care about."

With a nod of his head, Travis turned and headed down the dirt path, unable to stop a wide smile. "Let's go get a good seat in the ring before the auction starts," he said.

When he looked over his shoulder and spied Rafe talking to a few shady characters, Travis sobered. The group of cowboys huddled together across the way glanced in his direction, making awkward eye contact. Trouble was written all over them. No doubt nothing good was going to come of besting that cowboy. Nothing good at all.

AJ didn't wait for the last gurgles of the coffeepot in Travis's office to finish. She needed caffeine now. Carefully moving the carafe, she slipped her mug under the stream of dark jet fuel.

Once it was full, she raised the mug up and inhaled deeply before sipping. "I may live, after all," AJ murmured. Overwhelmed was her mantra the last week, yet she loved every bit of her job.

Being needed and appreciated was a good thing. She sank into a chair at the makeshift card-table desk set up for her and continued to work on the grant paperwork.

"You know what time it is?"

Too weary to be startled, AJ looked up at Travis's voice. The man filled the doorway and she did her best not to stare at his beard-shadowed jaw or the wide shoulders. That would make her as bad as Rafe Diego. Judging a person by their appearance. She'd never done that before. Never even thought about a man, like she did Travis. Despite her good intentions, thoughts of the tall rancher snuck up on her when she least expected. It was annoying. And it had to stop.

"You awake?" he asked.

She raised her eyes and took a generous sip of coffee before commenting. "Barely, and yes, I know what time it is. Close to midnight," she answered.

Travis chuckled. "Tripp's bringing Emma's horse back over from the girls' ranch for you in…" He glanced at his watch. "Six hours. He says Bess can board over here until the rodeo so you can get in more practice time."

AJ groaned. "This would have been good information to know before I drank this coffee."

"You can always find time for a nap tomorrow. That's what Saturdays are for."

"Oh, is that what they're for?" She shook her head and placed a hand on a pile of papers to the left of her. "I thought they were for going through this batch of job applicants. Thirty-six candidates. The ad appeared in the *Independence* on Tuesday. This is Friday. How can that be?"

"Tight economy. So, how do they look?" Travis asked.

When he slid into the chair next to her and reached for the paperwork, AJ moved her hand out of the way. But not in time. His big hand covered hers, the warmth wrapping itself around her like a cocoon, and she froze, unable, unwilling, to move.

Travis's eyes darkened for a moment as he watched her. "We always seem to be getting tangled up, don't we?"

AJ wished she could come up with a clever response. Not going to happen. The man left her tongue-tied so often she knew better than to try. She slipped her hand free and handed him the stack of applications while feigning a nonchalance she was far from feeling.

"I recognize a few of these names," he said as he flipped through the pages. "I might be able to give you some insight on their work ethic. Although, we've already established that I'm a push-over and you should ignore anything I say."

She barely held back a laugh.

He studied the pages for minutes and then frowned. "You put a call out on the cowgirl network?"

Surprised at his question, AJ examined the dark liquid in her mug. Travis had hit much too close to the truth. She actually had reached out to a few folks, but that was more information than he needed right now.

"Why?" she asked.

"Lots of female applicants."

"Is that a problem?"

"Not as long as they're qualified." He looked at her. "Keep in mind that we only have two open spots in the ladies' bunkhouse."

"We're only hiring two wranglers," she returned.

He opened his mouth and then closed it again. Silence stretched.

"How's the grant paperwork going?" Travis asked.

"Beside the fact that my eyes are crossed? Fine. I'm working on your cow day conversion stats."

"Aren't you using RangePro? You know Emma's husband, Steve, developed that program. I mean before we lost him."

"Lost him?"

"Car accident."

"Oh, so sorry."

Travis nodded. "If you have any questions about RangePro, Emma can answer them."

"Here's the thing, Travis. A cattle management software program is only as good as the information you input."

"Yeah. I get that."

"This hasn't been updated since you bought your first head of cattle."

"That may very well be true."

She frowned. "It's absolutely true. It's going to take me a bit of time to get everything up to date."

"Other than that, how are things looking?" he asked.

"Other than giving RangePro another forty hours of my life, everything is fine." AJ rubbed her head. "By the way, I'm looking into another opportunity."

"Oh?"

"There's another grant out there that you may qualify for. Smaller, but still an attractive opportunity for Big Heart Ranch."

"What are the parameters?"

She ticked off on her fingers. "A novice ranch or farm operation that strengthens family farming, has young people directly involved in producing, is part of an educational program, has a specialty product and women producers."

"Specialty product? What would that be?"

She smiled.

"Bison," he said flatly.

"And I'm your female producer. Hiring me and other women can actually help you nab this grant."

"Bison aside, looks like hiring you was a smart move."

She stared at him. "A smart move your sisters made. Correct me if I'm wrong, but I had the distinct impression you did not support that decision."

"Perhaps, but I've since come to revise my opinion." Travis directed his attention to the laptop as her words hit home. "Nice that we have so much grazing land, right?"

She nodded. "What would be nice is if Big Heart Ranch produced their own hay supply."

"Maybe next year. Not enough manpower right now. Bottom line is we can't have the ranch operations overshadow the kid operations."

"You're paying premium prices for hay. Another long winter and the kid operation may be kicking in funding to support the ranch operation."

She shoved papers at him. "Another option is pasture renting. Here's the stats on what's going on locally and regionally."

He glanced at the paperwork. "Next spring

we'll revisit this and decide what our next step will be."

"A year," AJ repeated. "Seems so far away."

"You plan on sticking around that long?" he asked.

"Let's worry about getting the grant submitted and take everything else one day at a time."

"Fair enough." Travis cleared his throat and shifted.

"You have something else on your mind?" AJ asked.

"Uh, yeah. I may not have mentioned the social. The one that's on the night before the rodeo."

"I know about the Spring Social. It's been a tradition as long as the rodeo."

"Great." He brightened. "Then you're going?"

"Of course not," she said, not liking the direction of the conversation. "Why would I go to a social?"

"I don't know." He raised his shoulders. "To be social?"

"Social is not in my job description."

"Actually, it is. As an employee, you're the face of Big Heart Ranch. Then there's that annoying fine print that covers this sort of thing."

"Does that mean you're going?" she asked.

"Everyone at Big Heart is encouraged to attend." The words held little enthusiasm.

"You didn't answer my question."

He ran a hand through his dark hair. "Yeah, Lucy twisted my arm and now I'm twisting yours."

"One big, happy, arm-twisting family."

"That's us." He met her gaze. "It helps if you try to remember that this is for the kids."

AJ sighed and leaned back in the chair. "I'm trying."

"I'm happy to drive you to the social."

"Then I'd be there without an escape vehicle."

Travis laughed. "True. A getaway truck is vital. I can understand that."

"When is this event?" she asked.

"Rodeo is one week from Saturday and the social is the Friday night before. There's a big firework show afterward, if that makes the situation more palatable."

She sighed and barely resisted rolling her eyes.

"The Oklahoma Rose Restaurant is catering and there's dancing."

"I don't dance."

"Nothing fancy. A small Western band. Made up of locals. Dutch plays the fiddle."

"I don't dance."

"Everyone dances. Some folks just stand and sway. Others do a little two-step. Or you can let your partner do all the work, dragging you across the dance floor all night." He chuckled. "Plenty of that going on."

AJ held up a hand. "I don't—"

Before she could finish her sentence, Travis had latched onto her raised hand and tugged her out of the chair and into his arms.

"What are you doing?" she asked as her heart thumped its own two-step.

"Proving you wrong." He nodded to the floor and tapped his feet. "Watch and follow my lead."

AJ stared at his faded, tooled-leather brown boots, right next to her own dusty Ariats and tried to ignore the fact that she was being held by Travis Maxwell. For sure, she was not going to look up. That would be a huge mistake.

With his right hand on her upper shoulder blade, his left hand held her hand at arm's length. Perfectly respectable, she noted.

Then why was she trembling?

"Real simple now, AJ. One-two-three-four. Two quick steps and two slow steps and we walk while we do that."

"Okay," she murmured, her eyes locked on his feet.

"You start right foot first. I start left foot first. Ready?"

She nodded. All her concentration was on his boots, even as his breath tickled her ear, reminding her of his too close proximity.

"Quick, quick. Slow, slow," Travis said time and again as they circled the small office.

She began to relax and leaned into his hand on her back as they repeated the steps over and over. Once she felt confident she could follow the steps and dare to look up at him at the same time, AJ did. The intensity of his gaze caught her breath and she stumbled.

"Whoa, there." He reached out to steady her and she moved from his touch.

They stood awkwardly, staring at each other for moments.

"Um, thank you," AJ finally murmured.

"You can dance, cowgirl," he returned.

"It was all you, Travis. I'm still not convinced I can dance on my own."

"Then I guess you'll have to save all your dances at the social for me." He winked, letting her know he was kidding.

"I… I better close things up and get going," AJ said. She rubbed her clammy hands on her jeans. "Barrel race training once again in the morning."

"Yeah, I'll be there."

"You don't have to do that," she said.

"I want to be sure you bring home a belt buckle."

She closed up her laptop. "I thought this was all about making a showing for the ranch."

Travis blew a raspberry and shook his head. "It's never just about showing up, AJ. It's all about winning."

All about winning? Like a game. And was holding a girl in your arms all part of that game? She pondered that thought with concern as she headed out of the office.

Chapter Five

Leaning over, AJ whispered in the mare's ear. "One more round and then we're done. You can do it, Bess."

"Come on, Bess," Travis called out. "Let's beat that last time."

"She can't listen to me if you're talking," AJ muttered from her position at the far end of the large corral. She glared at Travis as she prepared to guide Emma's mare into the final barrel pattern. AJ led Bess to the right side of the barrel. The horse relaxed and bent as they ripped through the cloverleaf course, circling the last two barrels with practiced ease.

"Whoo-ee," Travis hollered. He waved a stopwatch into the air. "Fourteen point five eighty-six. Nice job. Not too bad for a gal who started out rusty."

AJ patted Bess's neck and trotted her over to

the fence. "Well done, girl. Don't listen to him. You were never rusty, were you?"

Travis chuckled. "I was talking about you."

She continued to ignore him as she dismounted, offering crooning words of sweet talk to Bess. "That's it for today. You're ready for tomorrow's rodeo." AJ walked around Travis.

"Where are you going?" Travis asked.

"Anywhere but here. I've been working this horse hard for two weeks. We're done. I'm going to grab a hose and give her a cool-down and an apple."

Travis's jaw dropped. "We've got another hour until lunch. Why quit now?"

She kept walking, moving with Bess to the side of the stables.

"Are you listening to me?" he asked as he followed.

"Hard not to," she mumbled.

"Don't you want to win?"

AJ stiffened at the question, forcing herself to relax as she began to untack Bess. After she pulled the saddle and pad off the horse and carefully placed them on the corral fence, she turned to Travis, barely reining in her irritation.

"I thought this was all about a showing for the ranch. For the grant?" AJ asked. The words were slow and measured.

Travis pushed his hat back with a finger. "Sure, that's right. But there's nothing wrong with winning."

"So you keep saying," she said.

When he offered his patented smile, a sudden realization hit. His sister Emma had nothing on him. The Big Heart Ranch foreman knew how to finesse. Charm was his middle name and she'd best remember that.

"I'm thinking you could get in a short practice tomorrow morning."

"Oh, you do, do you?"

AJ tested the water from the hose with a hand, then ran an easy stream over Bess's hooves, acclimating her to the temperature. Circling the horse, she moved the stream up the animal's legs then watered down her flank and the rest of the mare's body in gentle movements. Bess nickered in appreciation.

"Is there a problem?" Travis persisted.

AJ turned with the hose in her hand and let the water hit Travis smack in the middle of his plaid Western shirt.

Startled, he jumped back. "Hey, cut that out, I'm getting all wet."

"That's the general idea." AJ cocked her head and nodded, pleased with her handiwork. "I'm thinking you need to cool your jets." She put her finger on the nozzle to increase the reach and force of the water and aimed for his hat.

"What are you doing?" A fast spray of cool water took the Stetson right off his head. He sidestepped away from the water and turned to watch his hat sail into a puddle.

"Bingo," AJ murmured. Her lips twitched and she leisurely targeted his boots next.

"Why didn't you just say so, if you wanted me to back off?"

"I've tried, but you don't take a hint. For two weeks you've done nothing but push, push, push. And now I find out it's all about winning? I don't think so."

"Okay. Okay." He inched closer, his eye on the hose as the water continued to splash his boots.

"Okay, what?"

"I apologize, and I won't pressure you any more about winning at the rodeo."

"I've been putting in twelve-hour days since you signed me up. This was supposed to be my day off."

"You can't blame that on me."

She released a short breath of disgust. "Bess and I are done. I'm going to town and I'm forgetting about barrel racing until tomorrow."

Moving even closer, he snaked his hand out and snatched the hose from her fingers.

AJ stood with her hands on her hips, daring him to water her down.

Travis held up a palm of surrender. He shook

his head in frustrated confusion and turned off the water, winding the hose up. Facing her, he cleared his throat. "So, uh, you have a fancy pair of chaps for tomorrow?" he asked. "Something flashy? Maybe bright pink?"

"No, my jeans will be fine. Besides, I don't wear pink and I certainly do not do flashy."

Travis sighed, long and loud. "Why am I not surprised?" he muttered.

The sound of his boots squishing with water could be heard with each of his steps. "I'll be rooting for you tomorrow."

"Fine, but root from afar."

"What's that supposed to mean?"

"You make me nervous," she admitted.

He frowned. "I do?"

"Yes."

His eyes met hers. "If it's any consolation, you terrify me."

AJ drew back at the words, unsure what to make of the comment. Was he finessing again?

"You still going to the social?" he asked as he picked up his hat and slapped it against his leg.

"I said I was."

"Sure you don't want a ride?"

"Very sure. I have other plans."

"You have a date?" Surprise registered on his face.

She murmured a noncommittal sound and offered a sweet smile. "I don't recall that my personal life being your business is in the small print of my job description."

"No. No. Of course not. As your employer, I like to be sure my staff is…you know. Just checking in to…" He waved a hand. "I have a civic responsibility to…"

"Easy there, boss. I'm doing fine. I appreciate your concern."

Taking Bess's reins, she turned and walked to the stables with the mare alongside of her, reveling in the fact that, for once, she got the last word with the foreman of Big Heart Ranch.

AJ circled the streets of downtown Timber until she finally settled on a parking spot beneath a streetlamp.

"I appreciate the ride, dear," General Rue Butterfield said. "Dutch will take me home. He had to arrive early to practice with the band."

"Oh, no problem." She hesitated a moment before continuing. "Mind if I ask you a personal question, General?"

"Not at all. I'm an open book."

"You and Dutch seem an unlikely pair. You're a retired army general and he's a cowboy."

"Therein lays the beauty of our relationship. We have only our love of Big Heart Ranch in common. Mutual respect is the key. Our foundation is respect and friendship."

AJ nodded.

"When you find the man who listens when you talk, you'll have found a keeper—like Dutch."

"A keeper?" Her thoughts skipped straight to Travis and the hours they'd spent in his office talking, arguing and finally finding middle ground.

Glancing down, she assessed her denim skirt and embroidered white peasant blouse. She'd even traded her worn Ariats for a pair of turquoise boots for the event.

"Are you sure I look all right?" AJ asked.

"Oh, my, you look lovely. And your hair! Who knew you had such glorious hair? You'll be beating the men off."

"Not exactly what I was looking to do."

Rue stared pointedly at her and frowned. "Why is it you hide yourself?"

"Hide myself?" AJ paused at the unexpected question.

"Yes. Underplay your appearance, as though apologizing for what the good Lord blessed you with."

AJ leaned back in the seat. "It's been my experience that ranchers don't like being reminded that I'm a woman."

"Any man who is threatened by your gender isn't really much of a man, is he?"

"I know you're right in principle, but that doesn't help my bottom line and I have the résumé to prove it."

"And outside of the ranch?" Rue continued.

"There is no outside of the ranch. I've never been real good with the whole guy-girl thing. I don't understand the rules."

"Ignore the rules, dear. They were created by men. You have to go by your instinct." Rue offered a kind smile. "I am certain that there is a man out there who will appreciate you for who you are, inside and out."

"I hope you're right."

"Oh, I usually am." Rue opened the door and scooted down, carefully adjusting her colorful broomstick skirt. "Are you ready to go in?" she asked.

"You go ahead. I need a few minutes."

"All right, but don't take too long." She paused. "You know, AJ, every trail has some puddles. That's part of life. But you never know what will be waiting for you if you're brave enough to face your fears."

"What makes you think I have…?" AJ's voice trailed off as she met Rue's no-nonsense gaze. There would be no wool pulling around this woman.

AJ nodded.

When Rue left, she stared at the Timber event

hall where the Spring Social was being held. The soft melody of a slow country song drifted to her ears through the truck's open window. She'd gotten this far, she would at least go in.

The plan was to make an appearance, taste the food, say hello to the other Big Heart Ranch folks and then sneak out. Quickly.

She flipped down the visor for a final glance in the mirror and reminded herself of Rue's words as she got out of the truck.

The lights in the event hall were dimmed and miles of decorative white mini lights had been strung across the ceiling, crisscrossing back and forth. The twinkling effect created a romantic starry night.

Red-checkered cloths covered the buffet table and shiny aluminum tubs filled with ice and beverages sat on hay bales.

Across the room, on a small platform stage, Dutch Stevens sat wearing a crisp, white, Western shirt and a red bandana around his neck. The crusty cowboy's head was down as he concentrated on his instrument. When he raised his head, their eyes met. A begrudging smile spread beneath his silver handlebar mustache and he raised his fiddle bow in greeting. Then he nodded toward the left.

AJ turned and immediately locked eyes with Travis who held court within a circle of women, all focused on the handsome rancher. His eyes rounded with surprise as he took in her appearance. She warmed beneath his scrutiny.

Lowering his head, he said something to his entourage. When he left the women, they glanced over their shoulders with curious gazes and longing side glances, along with plenty of hushed whispers.

Travis dodged the milling groups of people in the crowded hall and was quickly at her side. His smile kicked her heart into a steady trot.

Why was it this particular man took her breath away without even trying? It didn't hurt that he looked ready for another photo shoot. She eyed his Western shirt and bolo tie and black jeans. He was clean-shaved this evening, and even his normally tousled dark hair had been combed neatly off his forehead.

"Thanks for saving me," he said.

"I saved you?"

"Sure you did."

"From…" She paused to count. "Six women? I'm a regular superhero."

"Wow. That many, huh?" He shook his head. "And not a single one of them could speak without giggling."

"That's hardly their fault, Travis."

He knit his brows and frowned. "What are you saying?"

"You reduce women to giggling and speechlessness." She gestured with a hand.

"That's plain ridiculous. You don't do that stuff. You never act like that." He offered a crooked smile.

Tongue-tied, she opened her mouth and closed it again without uttering a single rational word.

"Did I mention how nice you look tonight?" he asked.

"Thank you." She folded hands together.

"Hmm." Travis glanced around.

"What are you looking for?"

"Your date. Is he the jealous type? I'd like to know if I'm going to have to eat knuckles for standing too close to you."

"I don't have a date."

"That so?" He perked up. "Then what say we find something to eat? I'm starving."

AJ turned, surprised at how crowded the room had become. "Which way?"

"Follow me."

She was caught off guard when he took her hand and led her to the buffet table, where Emma was waiting for them. AJ quickly tugged her hand free from Travis's.

"AJ! You look so nice," Emma said.

"Thank you. So do you." Travis's little sister wore a teal blue prairie dress cinched at the waist with a wide black belt.

"Travis tells me you and Bess are quite the team."

"She's an amazing barrel horse," AJ said. "Handles the ground really well. It's obvious you put a lot of work into training her."

"I haven't been able to keep up her daily drills the way I'd like to, but a few of the girls from the ranch have been helping me out. You're welcome to work with them. In fact, they'd love to have a trainer. I know you have a heavy workload with Travis. I hate to even ask."

"No. I'd really like that. I'll find time."

"They'll be delighted."

Travis lowered his head between them. "Ladies, will you excuse me for a minute? I see an old friend I'd like to harass."

"Go ahead, Travis. We'll just talk about you while you're gone," Emma said. "Your ears will be burning."

"I expect nothing less," he returned with a wink. "And could you try not to eat all the food?"

Emma gave his shoulder a playful punch. Her gaze followed his retreat. "The man claims he's an introvert, yet he's always right in the thick of things. Ever notice?"

AJ nodded with agreement at the astute observation. "Is your sister here?" she asked.

"No. One of the triplets isn't feeling well. But

she'll be at the rodeo tomorrow. You heard the big news?" Emma grinned.

"I did. Congratulations. So you're going to be an aunt again?"

"Yes and it will be a Christmas baby," Emma said. "It used to be just the three of us, all alone in the world, but the Lord keeps multiplying and blessing the Maxwells."

Emma's happiness was contagious and for the first time AJ found herself wondering what it would be like to have a sister or a brother. Jace had been a grown man when they'd become step siblings. If anything, he'd resented her intrusion into his life at holidays. What would it be like to be part of a real family again? The thought gave her an ache of longing. Was she destined to be alone forever?

A moment later the music began and an elderly, silver-haired cowboy came to claim Emma in a dance.

"Do you mind?" Emma asked.

"No. Of course not." AJ turned to the buffet table. She took a small white plate and evaluated the varied platters on the table before choosing a pastry.

The plump, elderly woman next to her turned and smiled brightly. Then she paused, eyes widening with recognition. "Jennifer?"

"No. I'm AJ Rowe."

"Oh, I'm so sorry. I'm Estelle. Pastor Parr's long-suffering mother-in-law."

AJ chuckled. "Pleased to meet you."

"I thought you were Jennifer, Travis Maxwell's fiancée. Silly me. I left my glasses at home."

AJ stood staring at the dance floor but not really seeing anything. Travis was engaged? Flirting with her when he was promised to another woman? Besides the fact that he was her boss and shouldn't be flirting, period, the startling revelation left her angry and confused.

She moved to the left when a cowboy obstructed her view of the dance floor. Glancing up, she realized that it was Rafe Diego.

Hat in hand, the cowboy bowed. "Ma'am, would you do me the honor of a dance?"

"I, um…"

He placed a hand on his heart. "Surely you won't hold my behavior at the auction against me. I certainly apologize."

"Are you bothering the lady?" Travis asked as he approached and stepped right in Rafe's personal space. Her nose was inches from the cowboy's.

"If I am, I imagine she can answer for herself," Diego said, his face reddening.

"Excuse me, gentlemen." AJ handed a surprised

Travis her plate and hooked her arm onto Dutch's as he passed by.

"That's a pretty slick trick you pulled there," Dutch said as he led her across the dance floor. "How come you're dancing with an old codger like me instead of a beau?"

"I don't have a beau," she said.

"Right." Dutch nodded. "On account of you being so hideous and having six eyeballs." He whirled her around and smiled. "And look at you. You can dance."

"Travis taught me."

"You're doing a fine job."

"I appreciate you helping me out, Dutch. I hope Rue doesn't mind."

"Aw, Rue and I are friends first. She won't mind."

"Why aren't you up there playing?" AJ asked.

"I like to give some of the new fellers a chance to shine."

The music wound down and Dutch released her. "Thank you, Miss AJ. Not often I dance with my boss." He scratched his head. "Truth be told, I ain't never danced with my boss."

"May I have this dance?"

AJ turned to find Travis at her side. "I, um… Probably not a good idea. You're my boss."

"You're Dutch's boss and you danced with him," he remarked.

"Fine," she returned, hesitantly placing her hand in his.

Before she could change her mind, Travis had an arm around her and they were smoothly two-stepping.

"Did I do something to annoy you?" he asked.

Arms extended, she stepped back, keeping as much distance as possible while she considered the question. Was Travis Maxwell another in a long line of bosses she couldn't trust?

"You sure are thinking hard. A simple yes or no will do," he murmured as he led her across the dance floor.

AJ slid another look at him. His personal life was none of her business. Travis was a charmer and she was no doubt reading more into his flirtations than he intended.

"Well?" he prompted.

She fully intended to keep her mouth shut but her brain disagreed with the decision.

"You're engaged. And I look like your fiancée."

"Whoa!" His head jerked back and he missed a step. "Who told you that? And, for the record, she's my ex-fiancée."

"The pastor's mother-in-law."

Travis rolled his eyes and said nothing.

"Does everyone think I look like her?" AJ's nervous gaze swept the room.

Around her, couples were moving back to the dance floor as the chords of a slow song continued.

"In so much as you have blond hair and blue eyes," he answered, "yes. But hey, if your last boyfriend had dark hair and dark eyes, I'd be a dead ringer, too. Makes as much sense."

"Except I've never had a boyfriend."

He blinked. "Never? Like the same never as you don't dance never?"

"Are you making fun of me?"

"No. Absolutely not. But you have to admit it's a little hard to believe."

"Why?"

"You're beautiful. That's why."

She turned on her heel and spun out of his arms. "My civic duty is done."

"Wait a minute."

She was out the door and across the parking lot before his long strides caught up with her.

"What just happened here?" Travis called from behind her.

Pulling her keys from her pocket, she stopped short at her truck. The streetlamp illuminated the fact that the rear left tire was flat.

AJ groaned. She kicked the rubber with her booted foot.

Travis knelt next to the tire. "That's one bald tire. You're fortunate it didn't blow while you were on the road."

She took a deep breath and said nothing.

"Come on. I'll change the tire."

"I'm perfectly capable of changing my own tire." Then she sighed. "If I had a spare."

"You don't have a spare?"

"I blew a tire in OK City and didn't have enough money to fix it and get a new suit for my interview with Big Heart Ranch. I've been running on a bald tire for a while now."

"Tough decision. That was a really good suit. As for the tire, we can take care of this after the rodeo." He held out a hand. "Give me your keys and I'll have Dutch get the truck towed to the ranch."

"That's not necessary."

"Do you plan to fight me on everything? Maybe you could pick a few battles to let me win. Just for fun."

She frowned and handed him the keys.

"Thank you." He turned. "My truck's parked over here."

The ride home was silent. When Travis pulled up to the admin building and turned off the engine, AJ reached for the door handle.

"Can you explain to me why you were so upset on the dance floor?"

"Look, Travis, I've been down this road before."

"What road?"

"Don't you think it's a bit odd that I look like your ex-fiancée?"

"Sure, but that's not my fault." He scratched his head. "I have no idea what that has to do with whatever road you're referring to anyhow."

"I don't want folks to get the idea that I was hired because I look like your fiancée."

"*Ex-fiancée.* And if you recall, I didn't want to hire you."

"Right. Right." She looked out the window. "How long has she been your ex?"

"Four and a half years." He tapped the steering wheel. "Listen, the truth is I was just arm candy to Jennifer. She's a rich gal who followed the rodeo circuit. When Jace was winning buckles, she was his biggest fan, and then it was me. I was too naive to figure out she was interested in rodeo glory and not me. When I left the circuit for Big Heart Ranch, she moved on to the next champ. Or, more likely, the next chump."

"She started the feud between you and Jace?"

Travis nodded. "Yep. That and the finals in Vegas. He lost the girl and the buckle."

AJ nodded. "Now it's all starting to make sense."

"What about you? There's more than thinking you look like my ex-fiancée, isn't there?" he asked. "What's the real story here?"

"Travis, I don't want anyone to say AJ Rowe is

the assistant foreman at Big Heart Ranch for any other reason than because I earned the title. Not because I'm cozying up to the boss or because I have a pretty face."

"You're talking about Rafe Diego?"

AJ shook her head. "There are Rafe Diegos on every ranch I've worked, along with bosses who are more than willing to cross the line."

Travis inhaled sharply, but she continued.

"Rumors spread faster than an F5 tornado and then I find myself driving down the road with my suitcase, looking for a job. Been there, trust me."

Travis opened his door. "You're working for me because, so far, you've done the job you were hired to do. I really resent any implication otherwise."

The words were flat, his eyes steely as he looked at her across the cab. After he climbed out of the truck, he took a deep breath and walked away.

Travis was mad. Plenty mad.

It was for the best, AJ told herself as she slowly eased down from the truck. She didn't need complications in her life. She definitely didn't need Travis Maxwell and the feelings he stirred up. All she really wanted was a place to unpack her boxes and put her hat. She prayed that, after this misstep with her boss, Big Heart Ranch might still be that home.

Chapter Six

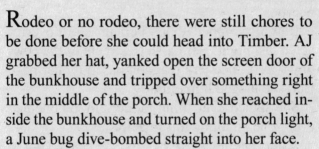

Rodeo or no rodeo, there were still chores to be done before she could head into Timber. AJ grabbed her hat, yanked open the screen door of the bunkhouse and tripped over something right in the middle of the porch. When she reached inside the bunkhouse and turned on the porch light, a June bug dive-bombed straight into her face.

Hands flapping against the insect, she nearly flattened the large, white, lidded rectangular box that was the reason for her stumble.

"I surrender!" She sank into the porch rocker and pulled the plain package into her lap.

Inside the box, a card was nestled in layers of white tissue. "'From Lucy, Travis and Emma. Thank you for representing Big Heart Ranch.'"

Folding back the tissue revealed butter-soft, parchment-colored leather chaps. AJ pulled them from the box. Show chaps with full rear fringe.

They came with a matching burgundy Western shirt embellished with pearl buttons.

"Oh, my," she whispered. The chaps alone cost more than her paycheck. Overwhelmed by emotion, AJ felt her eyes sting with moisture and she rubbed them with her fingers.

Dust. It was clearly a dusty morning.

AJ turned the card over. "'Your tire is fixed. Keys are under the mat. Thought you'd want to go to the rodeo yourself. Don't want to make you nervous.'"

Remorse nipped at her. Perhaps she'd overreacted last night. Her harsh treatment of the cowboy was a knee-jerk reaction based on her past. Had she judged him unfairly?

She sighed. One thing for certain, no one had ever done anything this nice for her.

After tucking away the gift, she headed out to the Ute.

Her heart was light as she led Ace along the fence line. The morning was silent, her only companion the pink glow of the sun as it stretched across the sky, waking up the day.

Daybreak continued to silhouette the conifers as she made her way from pasture to pasture. A sudden sound had her pull up on the horse's reins. She stopped and listened. The unmistakable sound of the metal clanging of an empty trailer bumping over the land filled the morning air. Who would be driving in the middle of the pasture at this time of day? Moments later she had her answer as the running lights of a vehicle glowed in the distance.

Straight ahead, another Big Heart Ranch utility vehicle was parked next to the fence. The closer she got, the louder Dutch's snoring became. The wrangler charged with night shift was asleep in the Ute, his head back against the seat and his mouth gaping open.

"Dutch, wake up."

The old cowboy roused enough to change position, his eyes never opening. "I'm not sleeping. Resting my eyes before the next set."

"Dutch, you aren't playing the fiddle. Wake up." AJ pulled off her leather gloves and tossed one at his head.

He swatted furiously and sat straight, blinking. "What's going on? Was that a hawk that attacked me?"

"Dutch, pay attention. I need you to call Travis and tell him to meet me out here. We've got rustlers. And then call the Timber police."

"You ain't going out there by yourself, are you?"

"Sure I am. Now call Travis."

"They'll see you."

"I'll stay behind the trees."

Dutch looked down at the glove in his hand and tossed it back to her. "No, sirree, I can't say I feel good you doing that. In fact, I'm sure Travis will have my head if he finds out I let you go out there alone."

"Dutch, I'm your boss. It's me you better be worried about. I have no intention of trying to take down cattle rustlers by myself, but if I can get close enough, I can see their license plate."

"I don't know."

"That was not a question. It was a direct order. Call Travis. Now."

"Yes, ma'am." He fumbled in his pocket for his phone as she turned Ace around.

She rode straight to a circle of trees and watched the burgundy truck and silver trailer parked smack in the middle of Big Heart Ranch pasture land. Cattle mooed as two riders moved the animals toward a ramp to load them into the truck. The men were tall and lean. No way was either of them Jace McAlester, but that was absolutely his truck.

AJ rode as close as she could to the truck, hoping to snap a picture of the vehicle from her position behind a group of trees. What would they do if they saw her? Chase her and leave the cattle? Maybe she'd be better off to find out where they had cut the fence and find a way to delay their departure.

"What are you doing?"

AJ turned to find Travis next to her. Her eyes widened. Normally neat and pressed, his wrinkled T-shirt was inside out and even his Wranglers were rumpled. And yet, Travis Maxwell on Midnight was the best thing she had seen since she'd gotten up this morning. Well, besides the chaps.

"How'd you get here so fast?" she asked, last night's argument set aside for now.

"Are you kidding? When Dutch told me what you were up to, I couldn't believe it. I nearly killed myself running across the gravel to the stable barefoot. Do you have a death wish? What if one of those guys has a rifle?"

"They don't."

Travis adjusted his hat and peered through the trees. "You don't know that."

"I can see that they don't." Indignation was definitely getting the better of her, but she was on a roll and couldn't stop. "You have a better idea, boss?"

He narrowed his eyes at her comment. "Yeah. I do. The Timber police are on their way. This situation has gotten way out of hand. I blame myself. I should have swallowed my pride and called them the first time this happened."

"It's not Jace," she said.

"Looks suspiciously like his truck."

"Doesn't matter. He's not there."

"Like you said. It doesn't matter."

The loud creak of metal as the trailer door closed ended conversation. The cowboys split up and began to walk around the truck.

"They're going to leave," AJ said.

"Can't have that," Travis said.

"What do we do?"

"I'll signal Dutch with my phone. He'll come at them from behind with the Ute. You go around the left side of the truck. I'll go right. Knock them to the ground if you have to. Dutch will keep them there with the Ute until Chief Daniels gets here."

AJ nodded.

"Here we go," Travis said, leaning forward on his horse.

Dutch revved the engine on the Ute and hit the horn.

AJ pushed Ace to a trot and then a full gallop, moving around on the left and taking the man on that side by surprise. When the rustler looked up and reached out to grab Ace, she stretched out her boot and kept moving. He fell with a thud.

"Way to go, AJ," Dutch called. "I hear sirens."

The two-man Timber police force drove across the pasture, bumping over the landscape. The white SUV moved up and down like a cart on a roller-coaster ride.

"So who do we have here?" Chief Daniels asked as he opened his door.

"Looks to me like Rafe Diego and his cousin Marco cattle rustling," Travis said. "Can't be sure with their faces in the dust."

Rafe raised his head and spit out dirt. "We

weren't stealing cattle. It was a prank. Jace McAlester offered us quick cash to move them somewhere else on your ranch." He pointed to the truck. "That's not even my truck."

"You cut my fence," Travis noted, his voice cold and flat.

"I'll pay for the damages." Rafe began to stand.

"Stay right where you are," Chief Daniels bellowed. He nodded to his deputy, who frisked each man.

"So this was a practical joke, huh?" Travis shook his head. "I'm not laughing, Diego. And looks to me like you aren't, either. But I imagine McAlester is."

"I trust you're going to press charges, Travis," the chief said.

"What's the penalty for cattle rustling?" Travis asked.

"The law says fines of three times the value of cattle, and up to fifteen years in prison."

Rafe's jaw sagged.

"Up to three times the value of the cattle, huh?" Travis looked at Diego.

"They don't make cowboys like they used to," Dutch added with a shake of his head. "In my day, they'd string you up for violating the law of the land."

"Yeah, but here at Big Heart Ranch, we're all about second chances. Technically this is only attempted rustling and, as it happens, I'm feeling benevolent." Travis pushed back his hat and rubbed the dark shadow of beard on his face. "How long can you hold them before I make a decision?"

"You know, Travis. It's the weekend. The wheels of justice move mighty slow on the weekend," the chief said.

"Good. I'll let you know if I'm going to press charges on Monday."

"Monday!" Rafe said.

"Yeah. Sure beats fifteen years in prison, doesn't it? Sadly, though, you're going to miss the bronc competition."

"That is a shame." The chief nodded.

"Real shame," Dutch chimed in.

"I leave them in your hands, Chief. Thanks for coming out."

Chief Daniels nodded and his deputy pointed Rafe and Marco to the police cruiser. "We'll process the crime scene and then you can have your cattle back."

AJ nudged Ace forward. "How can we help, Chief Daniels?"

"We'll need to count 'em."

"Dutch and I will assist," she said.

He tipped his hat. "Thank you, ma'am. Then we all can get back to preparing for the rodeo."

AJ glanced at Rafe Diego and his cousin. She almost felt sorry for them. Almost.

Travis paused to listen as the announcer's voice boomed overhead.

"Ladies and gentleman, welcome to the twenty-fourth annual Timber Rodeo. Timber, Oklahoma, is the home of the Timber triple berry pie. Stop by the Timber Diner today to order yours."

The crowd hooted and howled, drowning out the Timber band. Travis grinned at the enthusiasm. The citizens of Timber loved their rodeo. As they should. After all, the Timber Rodeo was the single biggest event in the town next to the annual Christmas parade.

Travis jumped up on the fence to watch as the grand entry began with trick riders carrying flags around the arena as the spectators cheered.

"'God Bless America,' everyone. Please stand for the national anthem."

The end of the national anthem marked the official start of the rodeo and the roar of the crowd swelled even louder.

"Ladies' barrel racing event is first up to the ground, and have we got a treat for you. A home-town cowgirl, Miss Amanda Jane Rowe—a former Women's Pro Rodeo Association finalist—joins us. Rowe represents Big Heart Ranch, where she's assistant foreman. That's right folks, assistant foreman. Today she's riding Bess."

"Say what?" Travis said aloud. AJ had never mentioned the WPRA. And he'd been pushing her like she was an amateur.

He shook his head and glanced around at the crowd. The bleachers were filled to capacity and the crowd cheered enthusiastically as AJ and Bess galloped into the arena.

Travis leaned forward on the fence to watch, his heart thrumming as horse and rider sped around the first barrel. Bess leaned into the pattern. The fringe on AJ's chaps fluttered as she sped like the wind around the next barrel. The horse led as they sailed around the third barrel and raced back to the starting point.

"Whoa, that was some ride. Wasn't it, folks?" the announcer called. "Ladies and gentlemen, thirteen point sixty-eight for Amanda Jane Rowe."

The fans in the bleachers stomped their feet, elated with her showing.

Travis tensed, his hands gripping the fence as the other barrel racers competed. After each performance, his eye went to the clock. AJ remained at the top of the leader board.

When the winner was called, his fist shot into the air.

AJ won. AJ won! He was beyond elated.

When she appeared in the arena with the winner's buckle held high and a wave to the crowd, they cheered and hollered with approval.

Somehow AJ's gaze found him in the crowd and she smiled, catching him and his heart off guard. He offered a thumbs-up before jumping down from the fence and jogging around the arena to find her.

Outside the stalls in the stable walkway, AJ stood, getting her picture taken and being interviewed by the *Timber Independence*. A line had formed with reporters from the *Pawhuska Journal-Capital* and even the *Tulsa World* ready to interview the winner.

When AJ saw him, she broke free and approached him, her gaze almost shy as it met his.

"Not all about winning, huh?" He took the show box with her prize-winning buckle and examined it from all angles before he wrapped an arm around her and gave her a hug. "Congratulations. You did Big Heart Ranch proud."

"Thanks, Travis."

"So why didn't you tell me you were a WPRA finalist?"

AJ shrugged. "And relive my glory days when I was fresh out of college? I don't think so. That was a very long time ago."

"Most cowboys retell their rodeo tales over and over."

"Yes, they do."

"Looks like you're a star." He nodded to the reporters who waited anxiously.

"They can wait a minute longer." She glanced down at the buckle in the box in her hands. "Thanks for the chaps."

"Oh, that was my sisters."

Her face fell. "You signed the card."

"It was me who told them no pink."

AJ smiled and ran a hand over the leather fringe. "I appreciate that."

"You look like the cover of *Cowgirl* magazine today."

A soft, sweet laugh slipped from her lips and wrapped around him. "Oh, no. Not me. You're the one who does magazine covers."

Travis turned to listen as the announcer called out a warning that the bronc riding event would be starting soon.

"Uh-oh, that's me. I better go."

"Jace is competing today," she said.

"Yeah, I saw his name on the program."

"You know you got this, Travis."

"I do, huh?" He looked deep into her blue eyes. Would he ever figure AJ out? Once minute she was putting up fences between them and the next she was rooting for him.

"Yes, you do. Bring home a win for the kids of Big Heart Ranch."

He winked and turned away. As he left, a petite

brunette with a wide-brimmed Stetson and pink-fringed chaps sidled up to AJ. "Wasn't that Travis Maxwell?" the other woman asked.

Travis slowed his steps, unable to resist eavesdropping on the conversation.

"It was," AJ said.

"He was on the cover of *Tulsa Now*."

"Yes, he was."

"Oh, my, my. I'll bet that man sure looks good in a saddle."

"The first thing you learn about cowboys is that there are more important things than how they look in the saddle."

Travis chuckled. Leave it to AJ to cut right through the cow patties. He broke into a trot as he headed for the chutes.

"Which bronc did I draw?" he asked, grabbing his saddle from the fence and hefting it over his shoulder.

The two lanky cowboys working the chutes for the Timber Rodeo looked at each other and grinned. Travis knew he was in trouble.

"Nightmare?"

Their laughter reached his ears and he groaned long and loud. The horse was the complete opposite of his ranch horse Midnight. An ornery bronc with a fractious temper.

"Are you crazy?" A too familiar voice spoke

from right behind him. "Why didn't anyone tell me you were riding?"

Travis turned and stared down at his sister Lucy. She might be older than him, but he had her by a good six inches, which helped when he wanted to be on the intimidating end of a discussion. This was going to be one of those discussions.

"It's for charity, Luce," he answered, skirting around her to grab his rosin.

"Getting yourself killed for a charitable cause? How does that work?" Lucy Maxwell Harris adjusted the brim of her black Stetson over her dark cap of hair and met his gaze. "Someone said you can't, so you just had to, right?"

He bit back a grin. She knew him too well.

"I paid the fifty-dollar entry fee, and they said I could ride one of those mean broncs. Simple as that."

"You haven't done saddle bronc riding in years."

"Aw, come on. It's like riding a bike."

"You weren't real good at that, either, as I recall. Broken arm when we took off the training wheels. Does that ring a bell?" Lucy shook her head. "And you're missing the point, Travis. The question here is not *will* you get hurt. It's how badly."

"Now, Lucy. Stop fussing. I'm wearing a vest. You and I both know I'll be fortunate to make it past the first hop out of the chute." He pointed across the arena to where AJ was still holding court, hoping to distract his sister. "Did you see AJ win that barrel race? She'll be on the front page of the *Timber Independence* on Sunday, no doubt."

"This is about AJ? You're trying to best her?"

"No, of course not. I represent Big Heart Ranch. All the other ranches are putting someone in the chute today. It's either this or the bulls. Take your pick."

She put a finger in the middle of his chest. "Fine, but if you're injured, I'm going to be very unhappy. Come Monday morning, I expect all parts of you to show up."

"Now don't get yourself all worked up, Lucy. You have a bun in the oven to think about."

She huffed at his comment.

Travis grinned. "Well, would you lookie there? My number is up. Time to ride." He twirled his sister around in a bear hug, set her down and jogged to the chutes.

Overhead, the sky was blue, the weather an agreeable seventy-three degrees as the announcer began his introductory spiel. A cowboy couldn't ask for a more perfect day to ride.

"And next up, representing Big Heart Ranch, is Travis Maxwell. For those of you who live in a cave, Big Heart Ranch is a local boys and girls ranch that provides a second chance to children in need. Maxwell, a former state champ saddle bronc rider, three years running, will be riding Nightmare. Let's see how this old-timer does."

Old-timer! He was only thirty-three. His boots weren't in the grave yet.

The announcer continued on, his voice bright with the same unbridled enthusiasm that stirred in Travis as he measured his rein before he climbed down over the gate to meet his fate. He slid onto Nightmare and grabbed each stirrup with his boots, tucking in tight to both boot heels.

"All Maxwell has to do is beat a score of eighty-five earned by Jace McAlester to ease himself into first place."

The crowd thrummed with excitement. Feet banged up and down on the bleachers in tune to the music.

"This is not the first time Maxwell and McAlester have gone nose-to-nose in competition, folks. The question today is, can Maxwell pull out a winning time?"

"Good question," he muttered. After a silent prayer, Travis offered the go-ahead nod.

Less than half a second later the horse turned out into the arena with Travis lifting the rein and holding on with one hand, the other hand high in the air.

"Eight seconds," Travis whispered through gritted teeth as his body waved mercilessly like a shaft of wheat in a storm. "Eight seconds. That's all I'm asking, buddy. Come on, Nightmare, let's get the rhythm. We can do this."

Forever passed by in slow motion until he heard the words he was waiting for. "Maxwell turns in what may very well be a winning ride on Nightmare."

The noise of the crowd going wild started closing in as Travis worked to dismount, and his hand caught in the leather. He slid from the saddle, awkwardly positioned between the animal and the fence. Nightmare took the opportunity to shove him against the metal bars with a resonating loud clang before kicking away, finally distracted by the rodeo clowns.

Travis was left eating red dirt.

"Whoa, that bronc took him to the fence hard there," the announcer said.

Travis spit out the dust in his mouth and rolled to his feet, struggling for a breath even as he plastered a smile on his face. The arena had become silent with tension. Everyone seemed to be waiting and watching.

"Looks like he's all right, folks. What a ride! Let's give that cowboy a hand!"

The hometown crowd roared with pleasure as Travis reached for his hat, dusted himself off and waved to the fans.

"Congratulations to Travis Maxwell who takes first place here today with an eighty-six."

"Yes!" Travis pumped a fist.

It was going to hurt like crazy to walk back into that arena and grab his prize buckle, but he'd do it and he'd do it with his head held high.

Limping off the grounds amid more cheers, Travis kept smiling. He took a deep breath and grit his teeth, tightening his jaw against the pain, though he refused to allow the grim fact that he'd probably busted his ankle as well as bruised a couple of ribs show on his face.

He stood, biting back pain, for the obligatory press photos and a quick word with a reporter.

"Could this be a comeback for you, Travis?" the reporter asked.

Travis chuckled. "No, I'm here to support the Timber community, representing Big Heart Ranch. My rodeo days are long gone."

"Well done, old man," a friend called out, clapping Travis on the back as they passed each other on the narrow walkway between the arena fencing and the bleachers.

"Thanks." Travis laughed and immediately regretted the action. *Oh, yeah. That hurt.* The pain in his left ankle increased with each cautious step.

Ahead of him, Jace McAlester stood talking to a reporter. Travis ducked around the bleachers. Last thing he needed today was a run-in with the ill-tempered cowboy.

Chief Daniels had left a message on Travis's

phone, letting him know he'd already interviewed Jace about the cattle and he claimed to know nothing except that Diego had borrowed his truck.

Yeah, the cowboy would be in a mood, especially after Travis had bested him in public yet again.

Travis's eyes rounded with surprise when he saw AJ waiting for him at the end of the walkway. Something about seeing her seemed right. Who else did he want to share the victory with? AJ understood rodeo, ranching and the pain of losing all that you held dear. When she stared at him, he found it difficult to hide anything.

Standing in front of her, he put a hand on the fence and did his best to pretend he wasn't in a whole lot of pain, hoping she hadn't noticed he'd favored his right leg when he'd walked.

"Nice ride," she said.

"Thank you," he answered.

No matter how much he tried, he couldn't stop the pounding of his heart when AJ was near. Was he falling for the prickly cowgirl? Surely not. He wasn't near ready for his heart to be stomped flat and kicked aside again.

"Not too shabby for a has-been cowboy," he added.

"Not too bad, period." Her fingers reached toward him and he froze as she gently plucked debris from his hair. "That's better, but you've still got dirt all over your forehead," she whispered.

"Do I?" He raised his arm to wipe his face with his sleeve. "Better?"

She nodded and glanced away.

"Can I buy you a Dr Pepper or something?" Travis asked, feeling like a teenager hoping to prolong the moment with a pretty girl.

"I'm a little old to be a buckle bunny, Travis," she returned with a wry smile.

"Nah. You're never too old for that."

Her soft blue eyes, fringed by thick lashes, rounded as she assessed him. "You're hurting big-time, aren't you?"

"Not big-time. Maybe a little."

"Define a little."

"Not so much that I wouldn't enjoy buying you a Dr Pepper. I mean, since you don't seem to be annoyed with me at the moment and I'm not annoyed with you anymore, either." He paused and looked at her. "Maybe for today we could just be two people at a rodeo not annoyed with each other."

She laughed and favored him with a smile.

Another wave of pain hit and he grabbed his side, bracing himself.

"Your ribs?"

"Yeah," he admitted with a grimace.

"Anything else?" she asked.

"Now that you mention it, I'm pretty sure I broke my ankle, too."

"Timber urgent care is five minutes away. I'll bring my truck around."

"Not Timber. Take me into Pawhuska."

"That's twenty minutes." AJ stopped and stared at him. "Tell me you're not doing this because you don't want anyone to know."

"I like Pawhuska."

"Seriously, Travis?"

"Oh, I'm real serious here." He closed his eyes for a moment as pain shot up his leg.

Yeah, a man's pride was a very serious thing. No way did he want to advertise that an over-the-hill cowboy was headed to the emergency room after what was no doubt his last ride.

Chapter Seven

Cupping her hand around her mouth, AJ peeked around the corner of the men's bunkhouse. She whispered into her cell phone. "Emma, this is AJ."

"AJ, is everything okay? I can barely hear you."

She glanced around once more before speaking louder. "I don't want to alarm you but I've just come back from the Pawhuska emergency room."

Emma gasped. "Are you hurt?"

"No. I'm fine. It's not me."

"Travis."

"Yes. He has a fractured ankle and some bruised ribs."

"The Timber urgent care wasn't open?"

"Travis refused to be seen there." AJ paced back and forth across the gravel.

"Why?"

"He won today."

"Yes. I know. Lucy and I tried to find him. We figured he was off celebrating."

"He was off getting x-rayed. Travis refused to be seen in Timber. He has a reputation to maintain. Especially since this was most likely his last hurrah in the saddle."

"Of course. What was I thinking? Macho mentality. I forget about things like that now that I don't have a man around the house. Where is he?"

"In the bunkhouse. Tripp and Dutch are watching him."

"I'll wake the babies and be right over."

"That's probably not a good idea. Travis is… well, he's not happy about being immobilized. I'm sure he'll be better after a little time to adjust."

"My brother spends way too much time worrying about what others think of him."

"I'm not staying in bed," Travis bellowed. The sound carried through the screen door to AJ.

Emma gasped. "Was that Travis?"

"Yes. He got a shot of something for pain in the ER. It's made him cranky and a bit confused."

"Oh, my. What can I do to help?"

"Could you let Lucy know? I mean, because then, technically, you told her and not me. He made me promise not to call Lucy."

"Oh, brother. And I meant that." She sighed. "Okay, yes, I'll contact Lucy immediately."

"Thank you."

"AJ, you better be prepared. Lucy *will* swoop in. Fast and furiously, too. She's a helicopter sister. Has been since our parents died."

"I appreciate the heads-up."

AJ put her phone away and snuck back into the bunkhouse where Tripp and Dutch sat staring at Travis. The man was asleep, sitting up in bed, with pillows tucked behind his back and propping up his left foot. His jeans had been sliced to his knee and the affected foot wore a soft cast. At the moment the only sound was his light snoring.

Tripp stood and soundlessly stretched his long limbs. He opened the door to the bunkhouse and stepped outside.

"How's Travis doing?" she asked Dutch.

"Quiet for the moment," Dutch said. "Conked out right in the middle of a sentence." He chuckled. "You go ahead home. Tripp and I will watch him. I can call Rue if there are any problems."

"Are you sure, Dutch?"

"Oh, yeah. You're going to need a good night's sleep. This entire operation is on your shoulders." Dutch grinned. "No pressure, huh?"

"Right. No pressure." AJ swallowed hard and planted a confident smile on her face. Dutch was right. Every single chicken, goat and steer on Big Heart Ranch was now her full responsibility.

"I'll head home, but first I'm going to fill his prescriptions," she said. "I won't be long."

She stepped outside where Tripp stood at the rail, looking out at the silhouette of the ranch at dusk.

"Nice ride," he murmured. "You did us proud."

"What?" She paused, confused for a moment. "Oh, yes, I nearly forgot. Thank you, Tripp."

He nodded and went back into the bunkhouse.

AJ smiled as she walked to the truck, feeling as though she'd crossed some sort of milestone of respect. Whatever it was, it felt good. Really good.

By the time she drove into Timber and back, Lucy's SUV was parked in the gravel area outside the bunkhouse.

AJ grabbed the plastic shopping bag and her canvas tote and started up the walk. Voices drifted to her and she stopped at the screen door, frozen.

"You don't have to stay in bed," Lucy returned. "You do have to elevate your leg and follow the doctor's orders."

"It's elevated when I ride a horse."

"That's not what the doctor had in mind. Besides it's dusk. Where are you planning to ride?"

"Dusk? What happened to the rest of my day?"

"You tell me. And why are you at the ranch instead of your condo, anyhow?" Lucy asked.

"My condo has too many stairs."

"Have you considered moving in with me for a while? The kids would love having Uncle Travis around."

"Kids. Right. Your place has enough kids. Besides, I don't need a babysitter," he growled.

"I didn't say you do. But we all need help on occasion, Travis."

"I don't need help, I need to get up and do my job."

"That's not going to happen until the swelling goes down and you get either a short cast or a walking boot."

"Not acceptable. What about the grant?" Travis said.

"There's always next year."

"No way. Do you believe in me, Lucy?"

"Of course, I do."

"Then don't even suggest I wait to get this program launched. This is my contribution to Big Heart Ranch and I'm not going to let an ankle fracture stop me."

"You could do paperwork," Lucy suggested.

"I'm lousy at paperwork. We hired AJ to fight that beast."

"Travis, AJ can't do everything," Lucy said. "Besides, she not only has your work and Rusty's, but there are interviews Monday for the two ranch hand positions."

There was silence for a moment and AJ took a step forward and then paused.

"You don't have to have surgery. Maybe you could be grateful for that blessing," Lucy said.

"How do you know that I don't have to have surgery?" Travis asked.

"I read your discharge papers."

"You violated my privacy."

"I'm your sister. That's my job."

"Lucy, I love you, but I'm a grown man. Time for you to stop mothering me."

Once again there was a long silence.

AJ turned and walked back down to the drive, not sure what to do. This was a family discussion and she wasn't family.

"You're right. You're absolutely right."

This time it was Lucy's voice that reached AJ.

Lucy chuckled. "After all, you did, so to speak, make your bed by entering the rodeo. I guess it's time for me to let you figure out what you're going to do about this situation all by yourself."

"Thank you, Lucy."

AJ turned at a sound on the gravel behind her.

A vehicle's headlights stretched across the grass as it parked. Rue Butterfield in the Ute. She got out and cocked her head. "AJ, is that you?"

"It is."

"Glad to see you. I didn't get to congratulate you earlier. You sort of disappeared," she said. "Everyone in town is talking about how Big Heart Ranch nabbed two first-place wins."

"Thank you. I have to admit, I forgot how

much I love the sport. It brought back so many good memories."

"What are you doing out here?" Rue asked as she approached AJ with a casserole dish in her hands.

"Eavesdropping."

Rue laughed. "Really? Anything good?"

"Travis and Lucy are about to start round two. I'm sort of scared to go in."

"Oh, that's just another day at Big Heart Ranch. Something would be wrong if Lucy and Travis weren't going at it. Come on." She balanced the dish in one hand and linked her arm with AJ's. "Let's storm the castle."

Rue marched up the steps, banged on the door and walked right in. "Dinner is here."

"Now that's what I want to hear," Travis said. "I'm starving."

"AJ," Lucy said. "Our barrel racing champion." She clapped her hands.

"Thank you," AJ said.

"And thank you so much for taking care of my brother."

Travis pinned AJ with his gaze. "You told her."

"No," Lucy said as she picked up her purse. "Emma called me."

When AJ placed the prescription bottles on Travis's bedside table and stepped back out of firing range, Lucy turned and put a hand on her arm.

"I mean it, AJ. God bless you for handling things because if it were me, I'd have tossed him in the creek three whines ago."

AJ smiled, her gaze moving from one dark-haired Maxwell sibling to the other. They were blessed to have each other. She'd give anything to be part of the camaraderie of siblings.

"Sisters," Travis muttered when Lucy left and they were alone.

"I wish I had a few. Possibly even a brother, too."

"Surely you have a few good memories with Jace."

"I can't say that I do. Besides, it's different. Jace and I have never spent much time around each other. I'm only family to him when it's in his best interest. You're very fortunate for the relationship you have with your sisters."

"You're right and I love my sisters." He gave a crooked smile. "The thing is, Lucy has been the designated adult since we were orphaned. She forgets that I'm not eight years old anymore. I have to stay on my toes or she'll be trying to dress me as well as doing her best to run my life."

She couldn't hide a chuckle at his words.

"What's in the bag?" Travis asked.

AJ pulled the trophy buckle display box out of her tote bag. "Don't want to forget this," she said, handing it to him.

Travis opened the box and ran a loving hand over the shiny buckle. "Can't say I didn't earn this beauty."

"The hard way," she added.

"AJ, are you staying to eat?" Rue called from the kitchenette.

"No. But thank you. I've got to get going. Early day tomorrow."

"What's on the schedule?" Travis asked.

"What isn't on the schedule?" AJ returned.

"So, you're sticking around?" Travis raised a brow.

"Was there a doubt?"

He shrugged. "I've had employees bail for less."

Travis was hurting and worried. She longed to ease the lines from his forehead. Instead she held her hands tightly at her sides.

"Travis, I'm not going to leave because of a little setback."

"I wouldn't call this a little setback. A pile of cow patties has officially been dumped in your lap. I couldn't blame you if you did take off."

"I'm not going anywhere," she said, her voice even and her eyes locked on his. "A cowboy finishes what he starts, and that goes double for cowgirls."

"Hadn't heard that saying before."

"Now you have. Believe it."

He glanced at his watch. "You'll come back and check in with me tomorrow when you're done?"

"I can call you. I'll be headed over to give Gus a workout tomorrow. Lem called and said Jace will be out picking up supplies most of the day."

"That horse again."

"I am completely loyal to Big Heart Ranch, but it isn't my whole life." She chuckled. "Only twenty-three hours of every day."

Travis looked up at her with soulful eyes. "I wouldn't mind if you were around 24/7, you know."

"That's the medication talking," she murmured.

"Is it?" His eyelids drooped and he was asleep again, his dark lashes resting on his face.

AJ stared at the handsome cowboy who had somehow managed to lasso her heart and was tugging on the rope. He needed her now, but could she trust that in the end he wouldn't change his mind and let her go? Only time would tell.

It was official. He was terminally bored. Travis glanced at his watch. He'd followed orders for seventy-two hours. No man could be expected to be still beyond that. He'd probably tied the Guinness World Record for cabin fever.

In between the fog of the pain pills he'd memorized the schedule for the Cartoon Network, watched a binge marathon of *The Tick*, and even counted the knots in the pine beams overhead twenty-four times. He was done with the pain pills and done sitting around with his leg in the air, like a trussed chicken.

Three days in isolation. Travis had to admit that he was disappointed AJ hadn't even poked her head in. Hadn't they mended fences at the rodeo?

He'd hardly seen Dutch or even Tripp, for that matter. Sure they'd texted him updates, but that was about it.

Though Rue came around regularly to check on him, the usual chatty doctor was tight-lipped. Even his sisters were more circumspect than usual. When Lucy and Emma stopped by with meals, the only thing he got out of them was that AJ was doing a terrific job.

If he was a paranoid man, he'd say something was amiss.

This morning he'd decided to attempt an escape. A hot shower balanced on one leg went pretty well. Now he stood on his right leg while rummaging in the drawer for clean socks. A glance in the mirror reflected exactly what Travis expected. He'd become a mountain man with a three-day beard. There was something primal about facial hair. He rubbed his face with his hands and grinned.

Actually it was not a bad look for breaking out of his log cabin prison. If he added a black Stetson he could do an aftershave commercial. He choked, laughing at himself, then braced his ribs with his palm to ease the pain. Yeah, the ribs still hurt but that was only when he laughed. Growling might not be too painful.

Picking up his crutches, he maneuvered to the bunkhouse door and took a look outside. The coast was clear. The enticing perfume of spring grass and sunshine teased him. A perfect pale blue sky overhead beckoned. How could he resist?

He couldn't. And that would be his excuse.

After hobbling to the Ute, he sank into the seat. It felt as cushy as a two-by-four and offered as much give. He pushed back the seat, carefully positioned his leg, half in the vehicle and half out, and headed to the road to check on the cattle. It took less than a minute to realize that the vehicle had the unique ability to find every bump, rut and rock in the road and Travis's rib cage felt each and every one.

He bit back the pain, sucking in his gut and holding his breath for a moment until he got to the east gate.

Pulling over next to the fence, he sat for a moment inhaling the fragrance of cattle that drifted on the wind. He could smell them, though he hadn't had a critter sighting yet. Cattle liked to hide in the trees and stomp through the pond, so where were they? Reaching under the seat, he pulled out his binoculars.

When a horse nickered, Travis turned his head.

Dutch Stevens grinned at him from astride his mare, gloved hands on the saddle horn. "They're out there. Don't worry."

"I wasn't exactly worried."

"Sure you were." Dutch narrowed his eyes. "Are you supposed to be driving?"

"Me? What about you? It's 7:00 a.m. What are you doing out of your cave?"

"I'm riding the fences. What does it look like I'm doing, standing in line at Starbucks for a mocha latte?"

Travis snorted. "You always told me your seniority earned you the right to sleep in."

"Tell that to AJ." He scoffed. "The woman doesn't believe in seniority."

"She told you that, huh?"

"What she told me was that if my name was on the schedule, I better get my seniority blue jeans out of bed and on a horse if I want my job."

Travis's eyes rounded.

"Tell me about it. Don't get me wrong. I like AJ, but that woman knows how to hold her ground. You don't want to cross her."

"You're not going to quit on me, are you?"

Dutch stroked his silver-white handlebar mustache. "No way. Things have gotten downright interesting around here. I'm looking forward to seeing what else the boss lady pulls out of her saddlebag."

"What do you mean 'interesting'?"

"You don't know?" Dutch's eyes lit up with amusement and he offered a snickering laugh that rolled into a full-on belly laugh. After a moment he wiped his eyes.

"Know what? What's going on?"

"Nope. I'm not going to be the one to tell you. You might decide to shoot the messenger. Besides, AJ said she'd tell you." He frowned. "I guess maybe she chickened out."

"Tell me what?" Travis fairly barked.

Dutch shook his head. "No can do."

"Try to remember that I'm the guy who signs your checks."

"And I appreciate it. But I reckon you need to drive that Ute on around and up to the north pasture."

"Dutch," Travis tried again.

"Sorry, boss. I got to get going. AJ's got me working from dusk to dawn. She's got some saying about eight hours' work for eight hours' pay. Craziest thing I ever heard of." He shook his head. "After I finish morning chores, I'm supposed to work on the fence in the north pasture. She wants it higher and more secure."

"You've had rustler problems again?"

"Ah, nope. That's not the problem."

"Then why does she want you to work on the fence?"

"Just go check out that pasture. Seeing is believing."

Travis grumbled as he put the vehicle in gear and headed along the dirt path to the north pasture. He didn't see a thing out of the ordinary.

A moment later two large animals lumbered out from around the back side of a large grouping of maple trees.

Bison. His jaw dropped and he stared.

Bison on his ranch. Two females. Because what he needed was more women in his life.

The nappy-haired beasts wandered around, making themselves right at home on his pasture, munching on his grass, forb and whatever else was out there.

"Travis? What are you doing here?"

He turned at AJ's voice. She galloped across the pasture on Ace. Her long hair was braided and hung over her shoulder. The welcoming smile she offered lit her face and warmed him, inside and out. He'd missed AJ the last few days.

Yeah, he'd really missed her.

That was a revelation he wasn't prepared for.

When the bison lumbered in search of forage, Travis's gaze followed them and he stared pointedly at the pasture behind AJ.

"Good to see you, boss," she said as she reined in the mare.

The words momentarily distracted him from the issue at hand.

"Uh, thanks," he said. The words came out more gruffly than he'd intended and her smile faltered.

"Bison," he said, pointing out the obvious.

"Aren't they magnificent? Sort of a reminder that the tall grass prairie is their home. Everything comes full circle with the return of the bison to the plains."

He crossed his arms. "I have to tell you that was not exactly my first thought. I'm trying to figure out what they're doing on my land."

"Now, Travis, before you get riled up, let me explain."

"Explain? Yeah, I was wondering when you were going to get around to that. I haven't seen you since you dumped me at the bunkhouse."

"I didn't dump you at the bunkhouse." AJ sat straight in the saddle. "And I was going to tell you."

"When?" he shot back.

"Today."

"Was that a question?"

"No. It was the truth. I've been real busy." She swallowed hard and fiddled with the reins.

"You had time to buy bison."

"It was on my day off and I used my own money. Winnings from the rodeo."

"Money you could have used to get Gus back."

"Gus isn't going anywhere. Lem and I have an agreement. Besides, I thought this could help us with the grant."

"Bison." Travis gave a slow nod, still not believing what he was seeing.

"Yes."

"Where did they come from?"

"I called around and found an auction house with excess stock."

"They saw you coming," he murmured.

"It was a fair price." Ace snuffled and two-stepped as her voice got louder. "Easy there, girl." She patted the horse's neck and crooned in her ear.

"They're eating my pasture grass," Travis said.

"Oh, come on, you have enough grazing land that we have options that smaller spreads don't have. Big Heart Ranch can easily support a small bison herd. Maybe as many as three or four. That's all you need. Besides, they forage differently than the cattle."

"I like cattle."

"If you recall, I told you about how beneficial the bison would be for the grants. You never disagreed."

"You took advantage of my failure to disagree. Is that what you're saying?"

AJ shrugged. "I did check with your sisters."

"Why didn't you check with me? I might have said yes." When pigs fly, he mentally added.

"I did stop by the bunkhouse. You've been mostly sleeping. I could have brought the bison to visit and you wouldn't have noticed."

"No. That's not true." His gaze connected with hers. "I did notice that you didn't stop by."

AJ's eyes widened. "Travis, ask anyone. I did stop by. Those pills had you knocked out the majority of the time."

"Hmm, maybe so. Seems my recollection is a bit scrambled. Stupid pain pills." He stared out at the ugly animals eating his pasture grass. "So Lucy and Emma are all aboard with the bison?"

"Sure, they think they're cute."

"Bison are wild animals. There is nothing cute about a wild animal on my pasture land."

She smiled fondly at the animals. "It's only two bison. Think of this as fostering."

He choked on a laugh and gripped his side against the sharp kick of pain. "Nice try. Big Heart Ranch finds forever homes for abandoned, abused and neglected children. We aren't a foster home to everything on the prairie."

"You have two goats living on the ranch who contribute far less to the future of Big Heart Ranch than these bison."

"Goats are educational for the kids."

"Think of bison the same way." She raised her brows as she pleaded her case. "I did call the grant committees. Both of them. They love the biodiversity we're developing on the ranch."

"Biodiversity." He gave a bitter laugh. "They come up with fancy new phrases every year, don't they? Do you suppose they hire someone to do that? That's a job I should have applied for when I was wet behind the ears."

AJ frowned. "As I was saying... Having bison pretty much clinches the grants, except for the walk-through. All that's left is to show a plan for tall grass prairie conservation and sustainable ranching. I know I've created more paperwork for myself, but I'm really enjoying this."

"Good to know someone is. And, by the way, we already have sustainable ranching. Another one of their two-dollar words."

"The grant committee is looking for evidence that we're ranching with an eye on planning, improving and reevaluating, all while taking into consideration the key economic issues of our region."

"Aw, that's a lot of malarkey. Though you are right about one thing. It's a good thing you enjoy the paperwork." He paused. "What about cattle reproduction?"

"What about it?"

"We have to either purchase a bull or think about artificial insemination, don't we?"

"Sure, we can discuss that when you're feeling up to it."

He shifted in the seat as a twinge of something like a hot poker shot up his leg from his ankle.

"Should you be out here?" she asked.

"I can't stay in bed forever."

"You're the boss, though anyone with any sense can see you're hurting."

"I appreciate your medical opinion, Dr. Rowe."

AJ jerked back at his words. With a cluck of her tongue and a tug on the reins, she and Ace did an about-face.

"Wait. I'm sorry." He was acting like an ornery old man in the face of her endless, cheerful optimism.

An awkward silence stretched between them as she slowly turned the horse around.

"Are you going to fire me for buying bison?" AJ finally asked. "If so, let's get it over with. I heard there was an opening at a big spread near Catoosa."

Travis released a breath as he contemplated her words. "I'd be an idiot to let you go. What other ranch has a bison nerd on staff?"

Her lips twitched as she gathered the reins. "There is that."

"And you got Dutch in the saddle before noon."

"The bison were easier to herd than Dutch."

Travis felt a begrudging smile coming on. "I owe you a steak dinner."

AJ grinned full-on, happiness brightening her blue eyes and once again causing a disturbance in the vicinity of his heart.

"Yes, you do."

"I'm looking forward to it," he said, meeting her gaze.

She offered a soft smile as his words hung between them. "So am I," she murmured.

"Soon as I can bear weight on my left ankle."

"Deal."

"How'd the interviews go?" he asked.

"Great. I hired two new wranglers. Stellar résumés and work history. They start on Monday."

"Anyone I know?"

"No. Although they both went to OSU."

"OSU Cowboys. Terrific. Who are they?"

"Josee Queen and Tanya Starnes."

"You hired women," he said dryly.

"I wasn't supposed to? You saw the applications and I don't recall you saying anything about hiring only men."

"That's right, because I didn't say that."

The air crackled with tension. "Then what's the problem?" AJ sat straight in the saddle, indignation all over her like a soggy blanket. "It's not as though your good-old-boy team was getting the job done."

Uh, oh. Now he'd stirred the beehive. And it didn't help that she was right, too.

Travis kept his mouth shut. AJ was spoiling for a fight and he wasn't willing to give her one. At least, not yet. His plan was to seize the day. Apparently he picked the wrong day. Maybe he should have stayed in bed.

Bison. It was all their fault. Things were going well until they showed up. One minute he was smiling into the pretty blue eyes of AJ and the next the massive beasts were in his line of sight.

"Aren't you going to say something?" she asked.

"I'm doing my best not to say anything you'll regret."

"You're mad," she said as though she fully expected the push-back.

"*Mad* isn't the word I'm looking for. *Annoyed* is somewhat accurate."

"Annoyed because you put me in charge and I'm doing things differently than you would have?"

Travis paused and met her questioning gaze head-on. She was right. That was exactly why he was annoyed. He wouldn't have had such a big breakfast if he'd known he was going to eat crow today.

"You're right," he said.

"Excuse me?" AJ blinked and cocked her head.

"I said you're right. Doing things the way I've always done them…well, it's provided a measure of control and security in the past."

"And now?"

"Now, I'm going to go welcome your new wranglers with Big Heart Ranch open arms and give them the same chance I gave Rusty."

Her shoulders relaxed. "Thank you," she breathed.

Travis shook his head. "I am teachable."

"I—I've got to get going," she said.

"AJ?"

Nosing Ace around, AJ's gaze rose slowly until their eyes connected.

Travis released a breath. "Thanks for taking me to Pawhuska after the rodeo and thank you for taking care of Big Heart Ranch."

"You're welcome."

For moments he watched her ride off, until she was merely a silhouette on the prairie.

Seventy-two hours was all it had taken AJ to whip Big Heart Ranch into place. Lucy was wrong. AJ *could* do everything. The woman was a born rancher, trained at her daddy's knee. Not only that, she was innovative. She made him look like an old rooster ready to be retired.

He could probably learn a lot from AJ Rowe. That is if he could find a way around his pride.

Chapter Eight

Travis looked up and down Southwest Frank Phillips Boulevard, assessing the storefront shops of Bartlesville. "They have great steaks at the Oklahoma Rose in Timber. Locally sourced beef. Why Bartlesville?" he asked AJ.

He stopped in the middle of the sidewalk as the answer to his own question poked him straight in the gut. "You don't want to be seen with me."

"We've discussed this before. It's not you. It's me. I'm trying to head off the rumor mill. I've been through this one too many times. I thought you'd understand. After all, you're the one who made me drive you to Pawhuska when you were hurt."

He sighed. "Yeah, I get that, but I don't like the idea that two friends have to hide the fact that they're sharing a meal. You'll sit in the office and drink coffee with me and talk for hours but you won't ever let me buy you a cup of coffee at the Timber Diner."

"What do you want me to say, Travis?"

"Nothing. I'm annoyed, I'll admit. Except there isn't much I can do about it until you stop worrying about what people think."

Laughter spilled from her lips. She cleared her throat and put a hand to her mouth.

"What's so funny?"

"I hate to beat a dead cliché, but isn't that…you know…the pot calling the kettle black?"

"It's different. I'm not ashamed to be seen with you."

"I never said that," she huffed.

"No, you didn't," Travis said, already weary of the subject. "Let's not argue. Okay?"

She nodded.

He offered a conciliatory smile that she returned. "I sure hope you're going to make the round trip to Bartlesville worth my while by eating like a starving wrangler."

"I can eat my weight in steak. Anytime and any day. And I'm looking forward to a baked potato with all the trimmings." She sighed. "I'll have you know that I haven't eaten all day in preparation."

"You need to get out more often. No need to starve yourself." He pulled open the glass door of the restaurant. "By the way, you look lovely. More than lovely." He glanced down at her patterned blue sundress and heels. "AJ Rowe ought to wear dresses more often."

"Thank you," she murmured. "My new roommates refused to let me out of the bunkhouse in my jeans."

"Remind me to give them both a raise."

"Oh, I will, I will."

He turned to find AJ peeking up at him through her dark lashes.

"What?" he asked.

"You look nice, as well. I've never seen you in anything besides Wranglers."

"If we're telling truths, you can blame Tripp."

"Tripp gave you fashion advice?"

"Unsolicited, even," Travis said. "You have no idea what I put up with between him and Dutch." As he spoke, his gaze assessed the crowd. "Pretty busy place, huh?"

"Friday night. It's date night."

Date night. He liked the sound of that. It had been a long dry spell since his last date. Nearly five years. Even he couldn't believe that. Five years was a long time to be gun-shy.

Oh, he talked a good show. Two friends having dinner. He was her boss and this was all business. But deep inside he knew the truth. There was something about this particular woman that stirred him with once-in-a-lifetime emotions.

Feelings that made him willing to take a chance, even if it meant getting his heart broken again.

A young couple bumped them as they squeezed past into the restaurant.

"Maybe we should have called ahead for reservations," he said.

"I made them," AJ said. "Under your name."

He shook his head. "How do you manage to keep on top of everything?"

"Oh, come on. It's a proven fact that women can multitask better than men. Something to do with the prefrontal cortex of the brain."

Travis arched a brow and stared at her. "You're messing with me."

"Not at all. I wasn't born with a messing-with-you gene. Remember, unlike you, I didn't have any siblings to harass or be harassed by. I was a studious, only child and I became a very literal adult. What you see is what you get. If you want someone to mess with you, you should talk to Emma or Lucy."

"Or Dutch," he said.

"Exactly."

He chuckled as he followed her and the hostess to a cozy table near the window where they settled across from each other.

AJ picked up the menu. "I forgot to ask about your ankle. How long will you have to wear the walking boot?"

"Four weeks, and then more x-rays and I may get promoted to my ropers."

"Wonderful."

"I think so. Limits my horseback riding, but other than that, I'm starting to pull my weight around the ranch again."

"A few days down and out with injuries hardly makes you a slacker," she observed.

"AJ, let's not fool ourselves. You're the one who's wrangled the ranch into shape over the last six weeks. Everyone knows that. You do it seamlessly, too, as though you've always been part of the Big Heart Ranch family."

AJ's face pinked at his words.

Travis only shrugged. "I'm not blowing smoke here. It's the truth, so why be embarrassed? Assistant foreman AJ Rowe gives each day two hundred percent. It's like you have a personal stake in Big Heart Ranch."

"I feel like I'm part of something bigger than myself at Big Heart." She folded her hands in her lap. "Do you know how many ranches I've worked?"

Travis shook his head.

"Thirty-four since I left home for college."

His head jerked back. "I didn't know there were that many ranches in Osage County."

"I've worked ranches in half the counties in Oklahoma."

"I don't get it. You're the hardest working employee we've ever had at the ranch."

"There's always a reason for me to be let go. Sometimes it's because I'm too pretty. Sometimes it's because I won't budge on my moral stance. Or maybe just because I'm too female. It never mattered before because none of those ranches meant anything to me. Until now, I never knew what it was like to feel like I've come home."

"Does that mean you're going to stick around?"

"Travis, it's never up to me," she murmured. "I can't say that I ever left a ranch because I wanted to. You have no idea what it's like to be a female in a male-dominated profession."

The ominous words left an awkward silence between them.

"Don't your ranch bosses stick up for you?"

"They've got a handful of angry cowboys who resent having to take orders from a female. If they get rid of me, all their headaches disappear."

"And the moral stance?"

She fingered the napkin on the table, her eyes hooded. "Oh, the usual. Being nice to the boss means job security. Or my last position where ugly rumors of favoritism by the boss bested two years of loyalty and hard work. I can't trust anyone to stick up for me when it isn't in their best interest. And it's usually not."

"I'm sorry, AJ. That's not going to happen at Big Heart Ranch. I can promise you that."

She simply nodded her head without responding.

"I mean it, AJ."

"I hear you."

Once their server took their order, Travis tried to lighten the mood.

"Hard to believe it's the beginning of June. Spring has gone by fast. We've only got a few weeks until everything has to be submitted for the grant," he said.

"I've scheduled a tentative walk-through with the committee people."

"Already?"

"Lucy told me that summer craziness starts July first."

"Did she mention that they bus in the kids from the Pawhuska Children's Orphanage each day for six weeks?"

"Yes, and I'm assigned a buddy. I'm pretty excited."

"It's fun. Exhausting but worth it. Each year brings a new adventure. This will be our fifth summer."

"So is it as busy as she tells me?"

"Busier. We'll have kids coming and going. The stables will be packed, as will the swimming pool and every trail on the ranch."

"Then it's good that I scheduled the walk-through for two weeks from now, before summer program starts. It gives us a window of two weeks on the other side, in case there are problems."

"Problems?" he echoed. "We're past tornado season."

"Even heavy rain could postpone the inspection. Any number of mishaps could be problematic."

"Unplanned disaster aside, do you think we're ready?" Travis asked.

"Yes," AJ said. "We've got this. It's eighty percent paperwork. The ranch itself is in excellent shape. I've never worked on a ranch more prepared. We're just waiting on your bull."

His eyes widened and he pulled out his phone. "I nearly forgot. I got a call while I was at the doctor's office this afternoon. We have a bull."

AJ's eyes brightened. "We do?"

"I've been talking back and forth with a small family operation located just outside of Pawnee, right off of Highway 64."

"And?"

"We came to an agreement."

She clasped her hands together. "You've seen the bull?"

"He sent me pictures, videos and all the stats."

"When do we pick him up?"

"'We'?" He grinned at her enthusiasm.

"You're not going without me."

"Wouldn't think of doing that. How about if we head out after church on Sunday?"

"That's perfect. I'm not on the schedule this weekend."

He smiled, reached across the table and took her hand.

"What are you doing?" she murmured.

"Looks to me like I'm holding your hand."

"You're my boss. You can't do that."

"No. I'm Travis Maxwell and you're my friend, Amanda Jane Rowe, and we're out on a sort of date, on a Friday night." He lowered his voice. "Is it okay to call you Amanda Jane?"

"Yes, though it's sort of a silly name."

"It's a beautiful name."

She cringed. "I prefer AJ or Amanda. Jace has called me Amanda Jane since the day our parents got married, simply to annoy me."

"I imagine just having Jace around was enough to annoy anyone."

"Tell me about it."

"Okay. Amanda. The point I am trying to make is that you are my friend. Not to be confused with my efficient assistant foreman."

"But this isn't a date."

"Details. Details."

She stared pointedly at her hand resting in his. "Do you always hold your friend's hands?"

Travis turned her hand over and studied each long, graceful finger. "This is a brand-new policy I've implemented. So yes, I plan to do it from now on."

He smiled and she hesitated for a moment before relaxing and smiling back.

Being with AJ felt right. She was a woman who understood his world, and they could talk for hours about ideas for the ranch or debate the merits of certain books and even politics. She had a strong opinion on everything and he respected her intelligence, even if she did champion those ugly bison.

AJ jumped when the door of the office swung open, banging against the wall. Travis stood on the threshold with a jackpot smile on his face. The man was cute when he was over-the-top happy.

"What's going on?" she asked.

"Natchez is calling us."

"Excuse me?"

"Our baby. It's time to pick him up." He tossed his truck keys into the air and caught them.

"Our seventeen-hundred-pound baby, you mean." She quickly straightened the paperwork she was working on and closed down the laptop. "I'm ready."

He adjusted the ball cap on his head. "My truck's over at the admin building."

"Do you want to walk?" she asked.

"Yeah," he called. He was already ten paces ahead of her even with a walking boot on and a limp.

AJ raced to catch up with him.

When Travis stopped short, she slammed into his back and stumbled, nearly bouncing to the ground. He grabbed her arms as she swayed and kept her on her feet.

"Are you okay?"

"Aside from those stars I see?" She blinked and looked up at him. "It's getting so I'm thinking of putting a traffic light on you, Travis. This is the second time you've failed to signal. Why did you stop?"

"Look," he breathed.

"What?"

"That." He pointed to a pickup truck parked near the chow hall. "Have you ever seen anything so pretty? It's giving me goose bumps."

"What am I missing here? It's a truck, Travis."

"That's more than a truck. A Ford F-150 Raptor Supercab."

"Whose is it?" she asked.

"No idea, but I like their style." Travis slowly walked around the massive vehicle, his mouth open as he inspected every inch of the exterior and crouched to the ground to peek at the undercarriage. "They call this the beast."

AJ rolled her eyes. "No kidding?"

"This is the stuff dreams are made of, AJ."

"A truck? You dream of trucks?"

"Oh, yeah. I've been saving every extra penny for five years so I can pay cash for one of these. I'm getting real close. By the end of the year I'll be walking into the dealership and claiming one of these."

"Exactly how much do they cost?"

He rattled off a number and she gasped.

"I hope you're planning to live in it."

"Come on. You're supposed to dream big. Otherwise, what's the point?" Travis turned to her and cocked his head. "What do you dream of?"

AJ frowned. "I don't dream."

He held open the passenger door of his old pickup. "That can't be. Everyone dreams of something."

Staring out the window, she tried to remember when she'd stopped dreaming. Maybe when her father died. It was so long ago she didn't even realize it had happened and she wasn't sure it mattered anymore. Yet, now that Travis mentioned it, the thought haunted her.

"We're almost there," Travis said as they passed the turnoff for Pawnee.

"Look, Travis, a produce stand. Let's stop."

"We've got to pick up a bull, and we grow produce at the ranch."

"Not fruit. This will take five minutes. Please. That bull isn't going anywhere."

"Five minutes," he grumbled. "I've heard that song before. I have sisters, you know."

The truck had barely stopped before AJ slid from the passenger seat and wove her way through the open market inspecting seasonal fruit. "Are you coming?" she called.

"Yeah. If you'd slow down."

"Fresh clover honey," she said, grabbing a bottle.

"You want a basket?" Travis asked.

"I don't need one."

"If you say so."

"Blackberries!" She turned to Travis. "Look at them. Huge." AJ put her thumb next to one. "Did you ever see blackberries that big?"

"Ah, not lately."

"Do you like blackberries?"

"In my pie."

"Me, too, and I make a mean pie. My mother was a blue-ribbon pie maker and she taught me all her secrets." She handed him the honey along with eight flats of blackberries. "Here, hold these."

"That's a lot of berries."

"I'll freeze them. Blackberry season will be over soon."

"Maybe I better get that basket." Travis adjusted his ball cap and headed in the other direction.

A few minutes later she realized he wasn't be-hind her. AJ backtracked and found him holding her basket of produce, being held hostage by three women. They smiled up at him as they requested his autograph.

He nodded and grinned obligingly for their phone selfies. When the prettiest one put her hand on Travis's arm, AJ's head jerked back as an un-familiar emotion hit her hard.

She crossed the distance to his side faster than Bess rounding the barrels. Looping her arm through Travis's, she gently tugged.

"We're late to pick up the baby, Travis," she murmured.

Before AJ realized what he intended, Travis leaned down and planted a soft, feather-light kiss on her lips. He raised his head, tipped his hat to the women. "Sorry, ladies, I have to go."

Shocked and speechless, her arm still locked with his, AJ glanced back at the women whose speculating gazes continued to follow Travis. It was a very good thing she didn't know anyone in Pawnee.

Still in a daze, AJ followed Travis as they paid for the fruit and wove their way back to the truck.

"What was that?" she sputtered as she fastened her seat belt.

"I'm telling you, happens all the time since that magazine came out." He polished an apple on his jeans and started up the truck. "Though it's a lot more fun with you around." He laughed and bit into the apple.

"You *kissed* me."

"Yeah. No one in Pawnee knows you're my assistant foreman."

She paused for a moment as she realized that she'd thought the same thing. "But—but…why did you kiss me?"

"Thought that might stop those women from following me around the fruit stand." He grinned. "It worked."

"But…"

"But?"

"Never mind." AJ sighed and turned to the window. Would he even understand that she was a grown woman whose last kiss was in sixth grade at a Valentine's Day dance? She'd spent the rest of her life on a horse or going to college. Or both.

She put her fingers to her mouth. That simple kiss meant nothing to Travis Maxwell, but it meant everything to her.

"Keep an eye out for Fisher Ranch. There should be a sign."

"What?" AJ swiveled around in the seat.

"Fisher Ranch."

"You just passed the sign."

Narrowing his eyes, Travis peered out the side window. "No. Not really."

"Yes, really." She pointed. "Back there, with the rooster weathervane."

Travis groaned. "Turning this thing around is going to take an act of Congress." Pulling off the side of the road, he carefully maneuvered the truck and trailer until he was going in the opposite direction.

"There. There it is," AJ yelled. "Oh, isn't it pretty?"

The butter-yellow farmhouse was surrounded with flowers. Colorful plantings ran the length of the front porch, hung from overflowing planters and circled the trees in the front yard.

Lush, freshly mowed grass encompassed another lot on the side of the little house and the other side yard held an enormous garden. There was even a hammock strung between two maple trees.

If she was a dreamer, this was what she would dream of. Roots. A house of her own. All her belongings in one place and no more boxes waiting to be unpacked.

"I see it," Travis said. "I'm going to back the trailer in so we can get out without jarring the bull."

"Nice job," AJ said when he'd finished.

When a tall rancher came up to the truck to greet them, Travis rolled down his window.

"Travis Maxwell?" the man asked.

"Yes, sir."

"Brian Fisher."

Travis jumped down and shook the rancher's hand before he circled around to open AJ's door.

"This must be your wi—"

"Assistant foreman. You can call me AJ," she said as she stuck out her hand for him to shake.

"Assistant foreman. Well, pleased to meet you, ma'am."

Travis looked at her as he held her door, amusement dancing in his eyes.

Would it be so bad to be someone's wife? To have kisses from a man who loved her? AJ touched her fingers to her lips.

"My wife is in the barn," Brian said. "We're bottle feeding a few calves."

"AJ, you coming?" Travis called.

"Yes. Right. Sorry, I was thinking."

She'd been daydreaming.

Flights of fancy, more like. Silly, ridiculous, unattainable imaginings, but it was a start.

As they walked down the drive toward the house, a small black-and-white dog greeted them. A puppy really, less than a year old.

"This fella is the last of the winter litter," Brian said. "We sold every last one but this little runt."

The dog raced in energetic circles around AJ's feet. "Oh, he's adorable."

"He loves the attention," Brian said. "Come on out to the pen. I have Natchez waiting for you."

A woman came out from around the corner and greeted them with a baby in her arms. "I'm sorry. I didn't hear the truck. It's been a madhouse around here with calves needing to be bottle fed."

"I'll bet is," AJ said. "I'm AJ, and this is Travis."

"Missy Fisher. Pleased to meet you both, and glad to get Natchez to a good home."

"What breed is this little darling?" AJ asked as she knelt to play with the little dog and rub behind his ears.

"He's what we call a hybrid. That's the politically correct term these days."

"Oh?"

"That means that his mother is a purebred border collie who got loose and we don't have a clue who the daddy is."

AJ laughed at the description. "I may have to take him home."

"Please do. He's yours. We'll call it a two-fer. Him and the bull."

Brian Fisher laughed. "Careful or Missy will throw the goat in there, as well."

"He's right." Missy nodded with enthusiasm. "You can definitely have the goat."

Travis raised a hand. "We have plenty of goats. Thanks."

The pup followed them as they walked over to the bull's pen.

"Let me grab Natchez's papers from the barn,"

Brian said. "You go ahead and inspect him up close."

"Thanks," Travis said. He walked around the pen and then stopped next to AJ. "You really want a dog?"

"I do. I haven't had a dog since I was a kid." She paused. "Are they allowed at Big Heart Ranch?"

"I don't think there's a dog policy. I like them better than bison."

She made a face. "Are you sure it's okay? You don't even have a cattle dog at the ranch."

"Omission, I imagine. Though this fella is a little young for a cattle dog."

"He'll learn."

Travis scooped the pup up and turned to Missy. "I think we're going to be taking him home with us." He met AJ's gaze and she was glad he couldn't see her heart melting at the gesture.

"That's wonderful," Missy said. "Seriously, look around. Anything else you want to take home, you go right ahead."

Travis laughed.

"If you can hold the baby, AJ, I've got a kennel carrier inside you can have for the ride home," Missy continued.

"Who's this little guy?" AJ asked when Missy put the baby in her arms.

"Max. Nine months, crawling like crazy and into everything. Do not let him grab that cross or the chain that's around your neck. He'll eat them both, and I do mean that." She smiled. "I'll be right back."

"Oh, Max, I'd take you home, too, if I could." The baby laughed and stuffed his fist in his mouth.

"We can take the puppy and the bull, but not the baby," Travis said. "I'm going to have to be firm on that decision."

"Very funny." She stroked Max's soft cheek then closed her eyes to inhale his sweetness.

"Ever think about having kids?" Travis murmured.

AJ's eyes flew open and she froze. "I don't think that far ahead."

"Not one of your dreams, then?"

"I told you—"

Travis raised a hand. "Yep. I heard you the first time."

Though, once again, for a brief moment her heart whispered that she was fooling herself. The image of a dark-haired little girl and a boy who looked exactly like Travis danced through her mind, leaving an ache in her chest.

"What about you?" she asked softly.

"I'd like at least six."

"Six? Oh, you can't be serious."

"I'm more serious than you can imagine. I want to adopt a few, as well." He winked at her. "You can pick your jaw up now."

Brian handed Travis the paperwork just as Missy came out of the house with the kennel. The two men walked over to the bull's pen.

Missy smiled, her knowing gaze going from AJ to Travis. "You look right at home with that baby in your arms. Do you two have any children?"

"Oh, no. No children. Travis and I aren't married. We're friends."

"Have you told him that?"

AJ glanced over at Travis. "What do you mean?"

"He keeps looking at you like he's afraid he'll lose you."

"Travis?"

"Uh-huh."

"Well, I have been known to wander off," AJ joked.

"Not anymore you won't," Missy said. "He's got his eye on you."

AJ blinked and pondered Missy's words while they packed up the truck and trailer.

"That was fun," Travis said as they waved goodbye to Missy and Brian and then drove along the long ranch drive.

"It was. And I have dog," she said, excitement bubbling over. She glanced over her shoulder at the back seat where the pup slept in the kennel.

"AJ, you're something else."

"I am?"

"Yeah. You're real. Genuine. You know?"

"I don't know anything else to be."

"Good. Never change." He smiled. "Though we're going to have to do something about your whole dream problem."

"I don't have any problems," she said with a laugh. "Now what shall we name the pup?"

"How about Oscar?"

"No. I'll think of a green puppet in a trashcan if we call him Oscar."

"Spot?"

"You're not trying," AJ said. "What kind of name is that for a cow dog?"

"If you want a proper name for a ranch dog, we'll call him Ranger. After the Lone Ranger."

"Ranger." AJ smiled and tried the name a few times. "Yes. I like that. Ranger," she called. The pup lifted his head and barked.

"He likes it, too," Travis said.

AJ was quiet for a moment. "The ranch dog I grew up with was my father's. He slept in the barn. I've never actually had my own dog."

"You've got this one. All Ranger needs is food and water and love."

"I can do that."

"I know you can." He reached out and covered her hand with his.

A sigh slipped from her lips as they passed the next mile marker.

"What was that big sigh for?" Travis asked.

"Today was really nice."

"Yeah, it was." He gently squeezed her fingers before putting his hand back on the steering wheel.

AJ peeked at his profile as he drove. Travis Maxwell was a good man. Prideful and stuck in his ways, but a good man. And in truth, he was the biggest part of what made today so very special.

How many good days would there be before it was time to leave? She didn't know, but one thing was certain: this time leaving would be different than all the other times. This time it just might break her heart.

Chapter Nine

When the door to his office opened, the aroma of something delicious wafted to Travis. He wheeled around in his desk chair in time to see Ranger trot in, followed by AJ. She kicked the door shut with her boot and placed the pie she held in her hands with a dishtowel on the corner of the desk.

"I figured it could finish cooling here. If I leave it at the bunkhouse you'll never see a slice. This is my second batch. Dutch stopped by when the first one came out of the oven and that was the end of that. Not even a crumb of evidence left."

When she smiled his gaze moved to her mouth. He'd lost a considerable amount of sleep last night thinking about a fleeting kiss he'd impulsively placed on those lips.

"Travis, are you there?"

"What? Oh, yeah. Sorry." He examined the golden-brown lattice that covered a mile-high layer of fresh blackberries. The deep purple juices oozed around the edges, glistening against the crust. "A blackberry pie, for me?"

"I told you I can bake pies."

"You certainly did."

She put her hands on her hips. "You didn't believe me, did you?"

"I am cynical by nature. Nothing to do with you."

"Why are you cynical, Travis?"

"You probably don't want to know."

"I do," she murmured. "You've listened to my tale of woe."

"You never told me a tale of woe."

"Sure I did. My background would make a four-part miniseries drama."

He laughed. "Not quite that much drama. Although your stepbrother could be a movie of the week."

"So tell me what makes you a self-proclaimed cynic."

"Foster care does that to you. Broken promises and then they shuffle you around like a game piece and every time you move you leave a little bit of yourself behind." He shrugged. "Which makes me wary and certain most folks are lying."

"I wish I could tell you that you're wrong, however if there was an organizational meeting of

Cynics Anonymous and they needed a president, I'd fight you for the title."

"Great." He laughed. "We're a sad pair, aren't we?"

"That depends on how you look at the situation." She leaned over to see the paperwork spread out on his desk. "What are you doing anyhow?"

"Well, um, I…"

"You know I've already filed all the grant application paperwork, right? It's a done deal."

"I know. I'm verifying everything."

"You're checking my work?" Her eyes rounded. "After all these weeks, all my work… You don't trust me to do the job correctly?"

He sensed the cold chill of tension between them as she moved toward the door.

"No. Please, AJ. I apologize."

She stood very still, her back straight. Finally she turned around.

"I trust you. It's me I'm having issues with."

"You need to turn it over to the Lord, Travis. Your value isn't measured by whether or not this grant comes in. Just like it isn't measured by your face on a magazine cover."

He nodded at the truth of her words.

"What's it going to be? Paperwork or pie? I can take it back home." She stepped toward the pie.

"No way. Do you know how long it's been since I've had homemade pie? Homemade anything?"

With his arm, he swept the paperwork on his desk aside and slid the pie right in front of him. "I'm officially forgetting about the grant. Leave this pie here. I'll keep an eye on it right in front of me."

"You're sure?"

"Very sure."

"I would have thought your sisters kept you knee-deep in home-cooked meals. And then there's the Travis Maxwell Ladies Swoon Society. Don't they cook for you?"

"There's a reason the Big Heart Ranch gate has a security badge entrance. I mean besides protecting the kids." Travis shook his head. "As for my sisters, if I give them permission to drop off cooking then they assume that gives them free range into my life. I'd rather starve." He chuckled. "Generally, I do, unless I stay in the bunkhouse. Tripp can cook."

"Tripp? Really? What does he cook?"

"Anything. Everything. And when I say he can cook, I mean he's like a chef or something. He has a huge cookbook held together by rubber bands and he has his own set of knives. Keeps them with his Bible."

AJ frowned. "I'm trying to wrap my head around that."

"Wait until Thanksgiving. You'll see."

"Thanksgiving is a long way off. I might compare pie recipes with him now."

"He might talk recipes with you. Tripp says you're okay and, from the horse whisperer, that's high praise."

"He said that?"

"AJ, come on, everyone likes you."

Flustered, she nearly dropped the towel in her hands. "I had no idea."

Travis broke off a piece of lattice from the top of the pie and popped it into his mouth. The pastry tasted like a television commercial. Light and flaky. "How is it you can bake like Betty Crocker and rope steer like John Wayne?"

AJ smiled at his words. "I attribute that to the fact that my father thought I was his son and my mother was determined I was her daughter."

"Leaving you with the best of both worlds."

"Finally someone who gets it. I get tired of explaining my many facets."

"I like your facets."

"Excuse me?"

"First thing I noticed about you." He pointed a finger in gesture. "Way back in your interview. You went toe-to-toe with me with bison and agriculture stats. You're an amazing woman."

A woman he could love. The thought crossed his mind before he had a chance to stuff it back from whatever hidey-hole it had come from.

"Are you being serious?" AJ rolled the towel in her hands into a ball and tossed it at him.

"What? I'm totally serious." When he pulled the towel off his head and threw it back, Ranger barked and jumped in the air in attempt to grab the cloth.

"How's your puppy doing?" Travis asked. "Have you got him herding yet?"

"It's been a week. I talked to the vet. Since we don't have an older dog to train him, he suggests obedience school."

"Sounds like a good idea."

"The local American Kennel Club in Bartlesville has herding classes, too." She sighed. "I can try to fit that in my schedule. Somehow."

"Or you can let Ranger be his cute self. He doesn't have to herd, you know. He could be a dog. No multitasking."

She raised a brow, obviously recalling their conversation in Bartlesville. "That option is becoming more and more attractive."

Travis broke off another piece of crust. "It's cool enough to eat now."

AJ chuckled. "You held out longer than Dutch did." She pulled paper plates, forks and cutting utensils from the tote she'd hung over her shoulder.

"What else do you have in there?"

"Vanilla bean ice cream."

"There you go, Ranger. Your momma knows how to serve pie," Travis hollered, setting Ranger off into a frenzy of barking and racing around the room.

She cut the pie and scooped up ice cream, then slid his plate in front of him.

"Lucy updated the Big Heart Ranch web page?" she asked, glancing over his shoulder at the laptop.

He looked up from the pie. "Yeah, and she put a video of you on the blog."

"Me?"

"From the rodeo."

AJ leaned closer in an effort to see the screen. "Show me."

He dragged his fingers across the touch pad and started the video. The rodeo announcer's booming voice introduced AJ before she and Bess galloped onto the screen.

Travis's eyes shifted again to his assistant foreman. He stared, mesmerized by her lips moving slowly into a secret smile of delight as she watched the video. It pleased her to no end that she'd won the event, though AJ would never admit to such vanity.

"Oh, that's actually sort of cool," she murmured with a chuckle.

When she turned her head and realized her lips were mere inches from him, she froze. He could feel her warm breath on his face and didn't dare move.

AJ swallowed as their eyes locked. Her blue eyes were wide with surprise.

Ever so slowly, Travis lifted a finger and traced her mouth, recalling once again the sweetness of the first time his lips touched hers.

She shivered and blinked as if coming out of a trance before she inched away. "More pie?"

"Haven't had a chance to touch this one yet."

"Oh, right. Right." Her face pinked. "I'll leave this on the counter and you can take it home with you."

"AJ," he said.

She turned, brows raised in question.

"Do you ever wonder? I mean, if you hadn't hired on at Big Heart Ranch and if we'd met, say, in town… Do you ever wonder…?"

"No. Never."

He didn't believe her for a minute.

"I don't dwell on maybes, Travis. I've found it's best to keep my hope in tomorrows, not yesterdays."

"Sounds to me like you've given it a lot of thought."

"No. Not at all." She gave an adamant shake of her head, causing her blond ponytail to sway back and forth.

The door burst open and Dutch stood on the threshold. His gaze went straight to the pie. He rolled his head and groaned as if in pain. "You got your own pie?"

"Yeah. I'm the boss. What of it?" Travis asked as he raised a fork to his mouth.

"Must be nice."

"Oh, it is," he returned around a mouthful. "Real nice."

"You ate almost all of the other one," AJ reminded Dutch.

"Not the same thing. I had to swipe it when you weren't looking. It wasn't baked with me in mind." He frowned and turned back to Travis. "Travis got one special, just for him."

"Mmm. Mmm." Travis smiled as he chewed.

"Boss," Dutch said, emphasizing the word. "We're ready to separate those mommas from the calves."

"Fence-line weaning?" AJ asked.

"Nah," Dutch said. "We just separate them so they can't see each other. We'll put them in different pastures."

She turned to Travis. "You've read the studies out of UC Davis?"

Travis gave a tortured sigh and raised his hand to stop her. "I've read it. You want to try fence weaning."

"I do."

"Portable fencing?" Travis asked.

She nodded. "We've got everything we need.

Well-maintained fences and plenty of water supply. And you know—"

He held up a hand yet again. "Did you memorize the entire textbook?"

"I have a good memory."

"That's what I was afraid of. Okay, we can give fence-line weaning a try."

"Thank you!"

"I'm willing to try anything that causes less stress for them and means I don't have to listen to bawling all night."

"I have my spreadsheets. I can prove it works."

"I'll bet you can, but it's not necessary." He looked to Dutch. "We'll move the herd to the pasture nearer the barn, so we can keep a close eye on them. Add some extra feed to the area and double up on the water supply."

"When?"

"Right after I finish my pie."

"I could use some pie before we get started," Dutch said. He raised his eyes hopefully.

"No way. That's my pie," Travis said.

The old cowboy grumbled under his breath as he reached for the doorknob.

"Thanks for giving my ideas a chance," AJ said.

He nodded. "I won't lie. I'm functioning under the influence of blackberry pie. Your good cooking may have unduly swayed my decision."

AJ grabbed the rest of the pie. "Have some more."

Travis grinned. There were some days when being the boss was particularly satisfying. This was definitely one of those days. On the other hand, being the boss meant AJ wouldn't consider dating him and that was a downright shame because remembering the brief kiss they'd shared was messing with his REM. It was a vicious cycle of interrupted sleep that he was going to have to deal with eventually.

Tongue out and tail wagging, Ranger jumped over AJ's boots and raced down the steps of the bunkhouse porch to meet Rue Butterfield. The general put down the paper bag in her arms and got to her knees to pet the enthusiastic pup. Dog and woman were silhouetted against a darkening June sky.

"This dog is just precious, AJ," she called.

"He's a charmer, all right. I've considered changing his name to Travis Jr." She shook her head. "Don't tell him I said that."

Rue laughed as she walked to the porch and placed the grocery store sack at AJ's feet.

AJ peeked inside. "Okra!"

"Yes. My garden runneth over."

"This is wonderful. I am all-in for any kind of okra. Pickled, fried, breaded and raw."

"That's good to hear as there is much more where this came from, I'm afraid." She offered a wry smile. "Oh, that my tomatoes were in such abundance."

"I just heard that Tripp is a chef," AJ said.

Rue nodded. "Something like that. No one has ever gotten the full story out of him. Tripp has his secrets." She pulled a red envelope out of her purse and offered it to AJ.

"More surprises. What's this?" She put her coffee cup down to slide a finger beneath the gummed flap of the envelope.

"Lucy asked me to give this to you. She always holds a small party for the Big Heart Ranch staff right before the start of summer. She calls it value-based management."

"We studied that in one of my business classes. It's a fancy word for bribing the staff, right?"

"Exactly."

AJ chuckled.

"Staff appreciation before the long six weeks begins. Lucy and Travis and Emma pass out the logo T-shirts we all wear each summer and there's always a nice little bonus in our gift bags. Think of it as Christmas in July. The party is held around July first each year."

"That sounds like fun."

"It really is. Everyone brings a dish and the Maxwells provide the main course and beverages. Just like a family get-together." She raised a finger. "You'll have a chance to see Tripp's culinary talent. Prepare to be amazed."

"I will." AJ smiled. "An old-fashioned potluck. We used to do that with the wranglers and their families when my dad was alive."

"Oh, dear, I didn't realize. And your mother?"

"I lost her in college."

"I'm so sorry."

"I appreciate that." AJ pulled Ranger into her lap. "Are you staying at the ranch tonight?"

"No, I came by to follow up with one of our children. He's fine. A rash. Nothing serious."

AJ nodded as she stroked Ranger's soft fur.

Rue slid into a chair next to AJ, an intense expression on her face.

"Was there something else, Rue?"

"I've been meaning to talk to you."

"Is everything okay with Dutch?"

"Oh, yes. I simply wanted to express what a wonderful job I think you're doing at the ranch, dear. Amazing really. It's equally hard to believe that it's only been eight weeks. Everyone is doing their job under your leadership and despite some grumbling…"

"Dutch," AJ chuckled.

"Yes, my old cowboy." She smiled tenderly. "Though he has a natural proclivity for sleep, make no mistake, Dutch has a great deal of respect for you. He thinks of you as the daughter he never had."

AJ bowed her head at the kind words.

"By the way, he's raving about your pie. He saved me a sliver. Delicious, dear."

"Thank you."

"And I couldn't help but notice that the new hands you hired have the same work ethic that you do. It's been nice to see Travis relax a little as the chores get done in a timely manner. A domino effect, really. When the boss is relaxed, everyone is, as well."

"Is the boss relaxed? I can't tell, because he still paces across the office every day worrying about the grant, triple-checks my work and calls me at all hours with panicked questions."

"That's just our Travis." Rue chuckled. "Despite his denials, it is clear that he and Lucy are absolutely cut from the same cloth. That grant is connected to his control issues and his pride."

"Oh, I can agree with that."

"Lately," Rue continued, "I sense his heart is softening. Perhaps he's moved past the pain of the disappointments in his past. I may be off-base here, but it seems clear to me that he's different when you're around. I wonder…"

"Oh, no. Don't go there, Rue." AJ gave a hard, fast shake of her head. "He's my boss. There is nothing else. Absolutely, nothing else."

"If you say so, dear." Rue patted AJ's hand. "But what about you? Are you happy?"

"Me?"

"You're certainly not the same person you were eight weeks ago. You've relaxed a bit, as well, and I couldn't help but notice you brought in a box and unpacked. Does that mean you're here for the duration or did you run out of clean socks?"

"A little of both."

"I hope you're giving serious thought to the future and are considering staying with us on Big Heart Ranch. We're family here and you've become part of that family." She reached over and rubbed Ranger's head. "Especially now that you have this little guy."

"I'm thinking about the future, Rue, that's for certain." There was little else she thought about lately. The closer they got to the grant approval the more her uncertain future terrified her.

"Courage is being scared to death but saddling up anyway."

She stared at Rue. Had the woman read her mind? Suddenly, AJ recalled where she'd heard that phrase and she started laughing. "You just quoted John Wayne."

"Did I?" She shrugged. "I blame Dutch. He insisted on a John Wayne marathon last weekend. I've been quoting the Duke all week."

"Oh, Rue." AJ chuckled and waved her hands in the air. "How could I possibly leave all this?"

"Exactly. We're a quirky bunch, but we do grow on you."

"I couldn't agree more."

Rue stood. "I better get going. Are you done for the evening?"

"I'm scheduled for the last ranch check and then I'm off tomorrow. Monday morning, as soon as the feed store opens, I'm going to bring grain up to my horse and give him a workout." She smiled broadly at the thought.

"I didn't know you have a horse here."

"He's boarded elsewhere for now."

"Why is that when you live and work here?"

AJ picked at a loose string on her Wranglers. "When I'm sure this is where I'll be a year from now, I'll bring Gus over."

"I thought we just settled that."

"I said I'd think about it, Rue."

"I won't press you further, though it's clear one of us has hearing problems and we know it couldn't possibly be me."

AJ smiled as the general took off with a jaunty salute and a wave.

The ruby lights of the Ute winked at her until they finally disappeared down the road, swallowed in the night's canvas.

A niggle of fear wound its way around AJ's

heart as she thought about the general's words. Yes, things were going really well, and that made her nervous. A gripping fear held her back from committing to Big Heart Ranch. Until she could move past her fear, all she could handle was one day at a time. That would have to be enough for now.

Chapter Ten

Travis drove the Ute around the ranch, doing the morning check of his part of the Big Heart Ranch.

Chickens, goats, cattle, bison and now a small black-and-white pup were his to watch over, and he was humbled by all that the Lord had charged him with.

The sweet smell of cut grass filled his senses and he drank it in. He shaded his eyes against the rising sun as he inspected the pastures. Straight ahead his cattle dotted the landscape.

One more week until the grant walk-through and then he'd be able to guarantee the future of the self-sustaining cattle program for Big Heart Ranch. He didn't kid himself about how that happened. AJ Rowe was the key to the success of the last two months.

He was beginning to rest in the confidence that the future of the cattle program was certain. Yes, he'd turned it over to the Lord, at AJ's suggestion. Now all he had to do was prove to AJ that he and the ranch were tied to her tomorrows.

Was he overconfident about that part? Perhaps, but he was fairly sure that the connection he and AJ had was worth investigating the possibility. He'd tried to show her that he cared, but the woman was prickly and it would take gentle wooing to convince her that his feelings were genuine.

Travis drove the Ute toward the north pasture, cutting from the road to the well-worn path across the pasture. Overhead there was evidence that the fence camera installation was in progress. Tall poles had been placed and at least some of the cameras had been installed.

When he rounded the bend, his booted foot slammed the brakes and he stared in disbelief.

Tensile fencing in the bison pasture was down.

This was a plentiful grazing area abundant with sweet grass. What would make the bison knock down a fence?

Didn't matter why. AJ's bison were loose. They'd trampled the metal and were somewhere on the ranch.

"Where the buffalo roam, huh?" he muttered as he got out of the Ute. Carefully protecting his walking boot, he stepped around the wire, examining what was left along the ground. Bison footprints were everywhere. There was no evidence anything had been cut. Jace McAlester and his cronies were not the culprits this time. Besides, Rafe Diego had been so grateful that charges hadn't been filed, Travis doubted he'd ever see the wrangler step foot on Big Heart Ranch again.

Tamping back the anger that was rising faster than he could think straight, Travis pulled out his cell and dialed AJ's number.

"Travis?" she answered, her voice light, reminding him for a moment of the Sunday two weeks ago when they'd shared the day together. A day when anything seemed possible.

Today seemed the total opposite. All that he'd worked for the last three months was on the line. He pushed aside everything but the task at hand.

"We have a problem. Get as many hands as you can out to the north pasture. Now," he said, not bothering with the details.

AJ arrived mere minutes later on horseback, concern etched on her face. She'd shoved her hair into a ponytail and her clothes were disheveled as though she'd thrown them on only when he'd called.

The rest of his ranch staff, including Tripp, was right behind her.

He heard AJ's gasp as she slid off her horse to examine the trampled wire. "Oh, no," she said. "How could this have happened?"

"You tell me," Travis said, his temper barely

restrained. "Bison. The ones I don't want on my ranch," he muttered.

"I checked those fences when I did rounds last night. Everything was secure."

"AJ, you and I both know that those bison may look cute but they're a danger to the kids on this ranch if they're loose. It's clear they took down the fence and right now they're a danger to all our animals and staff."

"Seven-foot wire fence." She looked up at him. "How did this happen without the night person seeing it or hearing something?"

"One person can't monitor five hundred acres."

"You're right. I still don't believe this happened."

"Doesn't matter what you believe. They're your bison. They're loose and you better find them and fast. I'm holding you personally responsible for this."

"I'm sorry. I'm so sorry," she murmured as if in shock.

"Sorry isn't going to mean anything if someone is hurt by those animals. Finding the animals is our first priority."

She closed her eyes for a moment, her face paling. When she looked at him, he knew AJ was thinking the same thing galloping through his mind like a runaway steer. Her bison could ruin the opportunity to obtain this year's grant if they didn't get a handle on the situation immediately.

Despair was on AJ's face and her eyes were distant as she faced him again. "How do you want to handle this?"

"Call Lucy and Emma. I want the entire ranch on lockdown. That includes the front gate for now. Explain the potential dangers inherent with bison. No one should approach the animals. This is not a petting zoo and they can be aggressive."

"Yes, sir." She mounted Ace and headed out without a backward glance in his direction.

Travis turned to his equine manager. "Tripp, shut down both stables until further notice. We don't need a horse gored."

"What about me, boss?" Dutch asked.

"Repair that fence. Grab Josee and Tanya and use the extra seven-strand high tensile we purchased for the bull."

Dutch nodded to one of the part-time wranglers and the two of them turned their horses around and galloped in the direction of the supply barn.

"Everyone else start looking for those bison. We don't stop until we find them." The staff dispersed as Travis continued to stare at the scene before him.

No, he didn't want bison. For good reason. The situation was a nightmare. He was going to look like a fool in front of his sisters, as well.

Travis turned his head when he heard the jingle of horse tack. Tripp.

"You need something, Tripp?"

The horse whisperer gave a nod toward the mounting poles. "Wireless remote surveillance."

"Yeah, I know," Travis said. "They're still installing cameras."

"Those particular cameras are functional. Wireless video and sound."

"How's it work?"

"They detect movement outside working hours, including night vision."

"Are you sure?"

"Yeah."

"How do I get a look at the feed?"

"Eventually we'll all have an app on our phones. Right now you can call the ranch security company. See if they picked up the playback from the camera company."

"I'll do that right now."

"Something is not right about this entire situation, Travis. No reason for two females to stampede. They have plenty of food and water. If they were startled by prey they'd be more likely to head in the other direction than take down a fence that size. I plain don't believe it."

"I guess we'll find out."

"And, Travis?"

Travis turned and met Tripp's unflinching gaze. The horse whisperer was not happy.

"You shouldn't have dressed AJ down in front of her staff."

Travis took a deep breath. "You're right. I'm sorry."

"You're telling the wrong person."

Travis rubbed a hand over his face as Tripp rode off.

It had taken him all of five minutes to overreact and open his mouth too far. Far enough he could have gotten his boots and his saddle in.

First he had to deal with the cameras and then he'd have to pray for a way to fix the damage he'd done to his relationship with AJ.

After calling the security company and the camera company and rousing them both way too early, Travis headed to the admin building. They had a representative to the ranch within the hour with a connection set up on Travis's laptop.

"Your security company sent us the feed they had," the rep explained as he typed a password. "Keep in mind that the cameras haven't been positioned yet. This one—the one on the bison pasture—is only grabbing the corner of the viewing target." He pointed to the time stamp.

4:00 a.m.

Tripp walked into the room and nodded a greeting.

"You can see the black-and-white night view of the side of a truck coming up to the fence. That's a male getting out on the driver's side. There," the rep said.

"Yeah, I see that," Travis said. "Can't see his face."

"He never looks at the camera," the rep said.

"What's he doing?" Travis asked. Then he answered his own question. "He's tying a rope on the fence and pulling it down with his hitch. Providing an easy exit for the animals."

"Doesn't make sense," Tripp said. "How could he be sure the bison would even be interested in going over that fence?"

"That's how." Travis nodded at the screen.

The video had clearly recorded the same person herding the bison out over the downed wire and to the road.

"You were right, Tripp." Travis shook his head.

"Are you calling the police?" Tripp asked.

"We can't identify who that is in the picture."

"You and I both know who it is," Tripp said.

"Once again, I can't prove a thing."

The camera rep stood. "Installation will be finished by the end of next week and then we'll need someone to work with our techs to adjust the camera view areas."

"Sure, give me a call when you're ready," Travis said. He offered his hand. "I appreciate you coming out this morning."

Travis walked outside with Tripp. The cowboy

gave him a meaningful glance as they stood on the sidewalk.

"I said I'd take care of the situation," Travis said, knowing exactly what the horse manager didn't have to put into words. He had to deal with AJ.

"Sooner would be better than later," Tripp muttered.

As Tripp left for the stables, Dutch pulled up in the Ute and hurried up the walkway toward Travis.

"Is the new fencing up?" Travis asked.

"All done." Dutch took off his hat, wiped his brow and slapped it back on again. "Had to go into town for more supplies, but it's done. No one is getting out of that pasture."

"Apparently it's not who's getting out that I should be concerned about, but who's getting in."

"That, too."

"And the bison?" Travis asked.

"Secure. They were walking down the road. No rush at all. Just walking," Dutch said.

"Where's AJ?"

"I don't know. Haven't seen her since this morning."

"Does she know we found the bison?"

"Yeah, she's the one who found them, boss." Dutch tugged off his gloves. "She sure was torn up. Blames herself for everything."

Travis grimaced.

"I tried to tell her these things happen. They're animals. Doesn't matter how high your fence is if they want to get out. They get out."

"Dutch, they didn't get out by themselves."

The old cowboy narrowed his eyes. "What are you saying?"

"We have video recordings. Someone let them out."

"Jace McAlester!"

"Maybe, maybe not."

"They going to arrest him?"

"We can't go around pointing fingers without proof."

"You did it to AJ this morning, boss."

Travis's head jerked back as if the words knocked the wind from him. He shook his head. "Yeah. I did, didn't I?"

Dutch gave a sad nod.

"I messed up, and I better find her before she decides that was her invitation to leave Big Heart Ranch."

"Things always look clearer on the other side of the saddle. You'll get through this. You need any advice on eating your words, feel free to give me a call."

"I might do that." Travis frowned. "Who's got night shift tonight?"

"I thought the cameras were working."

"Night shift continues until everything is tested and functional on all the pastures."

"Well, then, AJ is on the schedule."

On the schedule unless she'd already packed up and headed out, looking at Big Heart Ranch in her rearview mirror. He'd messed up big-time. This was far from his first time, but he couldn't remember when in his thirty-three years that he'd blown things quite this spectacularly.

He could only pray that asking for forgiveness rolled off his tongue as quickly and believably as his harsh accusations had this morning.

From bad to worse. AJ sat in her truck and stared out through the Chevy's mud-spattered windshield at the pasture. The only illumination was the waxing gibbous moon against a cloudy sky. Her eyes followed the crooked line of a crack in the glass in front of her. It nearly stretched across the entire windshield like a spider.

What started as a tiny little ding was now out of control. Way out of control. It couldn't be fixed. Only replaced.

The slight breeze that blew through the open window carried a thick layer of humidity. Maybe it would rain tomorrow. A cleansing rain was exactly what she needed to wash away the pain of this horrible day.

Her eyes were swollen and gritty from crying,

yet she stared at the bison until she'd memorized every inch of the silhouette of their shaggy bodies, even in the semi-dark.

Despite the debacle of this morning, she remained a staunch supporter of the beasts. Too bad there was no one supporting her. She'd been tried and convicted without a backward glance. Once again she'd misplaced her trust. The kicker was that this time her heart had been broken, as well.

And now in her most vulnerable moment she'd lost the only other thing she could count on.

Gus.

As she stared straight ahead, the conversation she had this afternoon with Lem played back in her mind.

"Lem, it's AJ. Is it okay to come by and ride?" She'd desperately needed her horse after the humiliation of the morning.

"Gus isn't here."

"What do you mean, he isn't there?"

"Jace sold him."

"How could he sell my horse?" She'd been near panic at the words and still was.

"He said he talked to you."

"No. No. He didn't."

"Well, he had the paperwork."

"Lem, that paperwork has been in my mother's desk since she bought Gus. All he had to do is look for it."

"Jace wouldn't lie to me."

"Momma bought me that horse. It's all I have left of her."

"Take it easy, girl. Don't get all worked up. We'll figure this out."

Figure it out.

Once again the pain punched her, over and over, until she was left battered and bruised.

Where was Gus? That's all she needed to figure out. There were half a dozen auction houses in the area. He could be waiting at a special sale, or already sold to the highest bidder. Or worse.

Gus wasn't young. Had her spiteful stepbrother sent the blue roan off to slaughter?

AJ swallowed hard and bit back the awful despair that threatened.

Deep breath. Deep breath. You've been through worse, she told herself. But she hadn't, not really. Each loss was more painful than the next. Travis broke her heart and losing Gus was about to break her spirit.

The blue roan was all she had left.

She whispered a silent prayer. A plea. All she could do now was trust in the Lord. No one else was going to save her or Gus. No one else cared about a second-chance cowgirl.

A glance at her phone said it was midnight. There was a job to do. The bison would not be leaving the pasture on her watch. AJ stretched her neck back and forth and twisted slightly in the seat, easing the muscles in her back.

The sound of a vehicle approaching had her turning around in her seat. The Ute. Its lights blinded her and she held up a hand to shield her eyes.

Travis.

Five hundred acres and she couldn't find a place to grieve in peace?

After a double knock of greeting on the outside of the truck Travis stuck his head in the cab. "Mind if I join you?"

AJ raised a hand in numb indifference.

Travis eased into the truck and shut the door. The man sucked up every inch of space in the cab with his presence. AJ scooted over until she was hugging the door.

Today's other pain sat inches away staring at her. His face wore what any other day she would have thought was concern. Not after this morning.

When their eyes connected, all she felt was disappointment for letting herself be fooled into complacency again.

"What are you doing here?" Her gaze skipped over him and then back out the window again, to keep her eye on the bison.

"I'm here to apologize."

"At midnight?"

"Best time. No interruptions."

"Have at it and then, if you don't mind, I have a job to do here."

He pointed to the tall poles outside the truck. "Those cameras up there recorded the bison this morning at 4:00 a.m. That's the time they got out."

She turned to face him. "What?"

"I'll explain how it works later, but the bottom line is we have recorded video showing someone taking down the fence and leading the bison out."

Her eyes rounded. "Someone?" AJ said the word slowly.

"We can't identify him."

"Him, meaning Jace?"

"Probably."

"So you're only here because you have proof I wasn't at fault?"

"No. That's not why I'm here."

AJ shrugged and rubbed her aching eyes. "Sounds like it to me," she muttered.

"Have you been crying?" Travis asked, his voice low and anxious as he peered closer.

She refused to meet his gaze. There was no way she'd be taken in by the Travis Maxwell charm again in this lifetime. The key was to avoid looking into those dark eyes.

"Don't flatter yourself. If I've been crying it would be about a horse, not a cowboy."

"Gus? Did something happen to Gus?"

AJ gripped the steering wheel. "Is there something else I can do for you, Travis?"

"You're not making this easy."

She shrugged. "I didn't realize I was supposed to make it easy for you."

"You're twisting my words around."

"You certainly didn't have a problem with words this morning."

He hung his head for a moment and took a deep breath.

"You're right and I'm ashamed of myself. I don't expect you to forgive me right now, but I want you to know that I am aware my behavior was out of line and I deeply regret my words and, worse, my thoughts."

"Okay, then. Thank you for that." She put her hands in her lap.

"Are you going to quit?"

"I hired on to do a job and that job isn't complete yet. We have another week to get ready for the grant committee walk-through. I won't let you down."

"It never occurred to me that you would let me down."

"Sure it did," she murmured. "That's why you asked if I was going to quit. Everything is about you and this grant and your pride and reputation. Someday you're going to realize you don't need to prove anything to anybody."

"The same could be said of you, AJ."

"Oh, no. You and I are very different. My pride disappeared a long time ago." She looked at him and gave a sad shake of her head. "I spend all my time wondering which hoop I'll have to jump through today and what test is next. I thought that ended here when I arrived at Big Heart Ranch. But today you proved me wrong again."

"Are you sure you aren't looking to be proved wrong? You can't go back to your father's ranch. Maybe you don't want to be happy anywhere else."

She glanced at her watch and reached for her thermos. "Are we going to psychoanalyze each other all night? If so, I guess now is as good a time as any for a strong cup of coffee."

"I came here to apologize."

"Mission accomplished."

His expression faltered for a brief moment. "Oh, AJ. How am I going to get through to you?" The words were barely a whisper as he opened the door and slid out.

Outside she could hear the mating duet of the hoot owls.

She rolled down the window and let the full night breeze soothe her. Except that it didn't. Nothing could soothe what hurt tonight. Nothing.

She'd spent a lifetime giving up things. This

was the first time since her parents died that what she lost really mattered. It would be a very long time before she got over Travis Maxwell's betrayal.

Chapter Eleven

Déjà vu at Big Heart Ranch. Here she was again pulling her thermos out of her backpack at midnight. AJ placed it on the passenger seat for later. This was the fifth night in a row she'd sat out all night in her truck. She didn't care if the cameras were in place. The bison were her responsibility and until the grant walk-through and approval she'd be babysitting them. There would be no repeat of the other night.

Overhead a full moon and clear sky illuminated the land. Something in her favor at least.

It was Friday night. Date night, she'd told Travis the night they'd gone to dinner. That seemed a lifetime ago.

She nearly laughed out loud at the irony. Never in a heartbeat would she have guessed that the sweetness of that long-ago evening in Bartlesville would be followed by the darkness of this week.

Shifting in her seat, her muscles searched for the elusive sweet spot, a position that was comfortable enough to rest. This was getting old. Next time she'd buy an old Caddy with a couch and a cup holder in the front seat.

She had sore muscles from sleeping sitting up and aches where she didn't know she could have aches. But she'd do whatever she had to do to stop Jace McAlester once and for all.

Jace typically hit the ranch Friday, Saturday or Sunday when staffing was low. She was ready for him. And Big Heart Ranch was one step ahead because Jace didn't know about the cameras. At Travis's directive, the camera company had put in overtime to get them all installed. Every last pasture had at least one camera set up and tested. Each recording angle had been reviewed and finetuned. If they could pick up a gopher dancing across the pasture, they could pick up Jace.

She reviewed the camera app feature on her phone, bringing up each of the pasture cameras one by one, then sliding the image to the left until she'd seen them all. The night-vision view offered a black-and-white visual and verified that nothing unusual was going on. Cattle standing in the pasture and newly weaned calves on the fence line. The bison were still and even Natchez stood motionless in his pasture.

Each day she was closer to the grant walk-through and the likelihood everything would occur on schedule without incident. Even the weather had cooperated with a stunning forecast of sunny skies, moderate humidity and not a chance of precipitation. Oklahoma in the spring. Mother Nature's very finest.

AJ sank low in the seat and pulled her ball cap over her eyes. The phone app would let her know when someone or something triggered the cameras, and her windows were open to catch any sounds in the night.

She was nearly delirious from lack of sleep and too stubborn to quit now. Not that she'd get any rest at home. Lying awake at night fretting about Gus, her questionable future and thinking about Travis Maxwell was enough to make her pace the floor.

Jace McAlester had stolen Gus, but she wasn't going to let him take anything else. She'd finish her stint at Big Heart Ranch with the knowledge that she'd done an exemplary job. Then she'd walk away.

Her eyes had barely drifted closed when her phone beeped and vibrated in her pocket.

Motion alert!

AJ shot up in the seat, once again hitting her head on the ceiling of the truck. There was someone out there. If her cell was going off, so were the phones that belonged to the rest of the equestrian and livestock wranglers, along with Travis and Tripp. She wouldn't be the only staff member following up. But she'd be the first on scene. The first one to nab the intruder.

She fiddled with the phone, bringing up the camera's event feed.

Natchez's pasture. There was movement near the bull's paddock gate. She could only see a truck pull up to the fence. It couldn't be staff this time of night. Only a cattle rustler would be at the fence and in the camera's eye.

"I've got you, Jace McAlester, and this time you're going to jail."

AJ locked her truck and tucked her keys and phone in her pocket. It took her fifteen minutes of jogging to cross the pasture to the field where the bull grazed.

Jace's burgundy pickup was parked along the dirt trail. She could see his form on the other side of the paddock, next to the gate.

Reaching in through the open window of Jace's truck, she grabbed his keys and pocketed them. Carefully opening the truck door, she climbed in and removed his rifle from the back window rack. She pulled back on the magazine and cycled the charging handle to release any remaining cartridges and carefully placed the rifle in the bed of the pickup.

A sound had her whirling around. Travis Maxwell stood behind her.

"What are you doing here?" he whispered. "You aren't on call tonight."

"I'm on self-appointed, on-call night-shift duty until the walk-through."

"That's unnecessary."

"Not from where I stand it isn't."

"You can't work night and day."

"Watch me."

"AJ, I was wrong. I'm sorry."

She ignored him and inched to the front of the truck.

"Look, could we agree to a truce for tonight? Until this little adventure is over?" he whispered.

Her only response was a grunt.

"I'm going to take that as consent." He moved past her and glanced around. "So where's our rustler? Are we sure it's Jace?"

"There he is." She pointed. "The man is the size of a refrigerator. That is Jace McAlester, all right."

Travis nodded. "He's got wire cutters in his hand. We need to catch him in the act."

"What do you want to do?"

"Nothing," Travis said. "Let him cut the fence, otherwise all we have him for is trespassing."

"Okay, and then what?"

"I'll get Jace and you get the bull."

"I'd rather do it the other way around," she admitted.

"I feel the need to protect you from yourself. You take care of the bull and I'll take care of Jace. He may never know that I saved his life tonight."

She turned to him. "Did you actually call the police this time?"

"Oh, you bet I did," Travis said. "And Dutch and Tripp should be here in a minute, as well." He nodded toward their rustler. "He just snipped the wire. Here we go. Approach from either side. That worked well for us before."

"Jace," Travis called.

Jace McAlester froze. He turned around, dropped the wire cutters and started running like a mountain man of a quarterback headed for the goal line in the last minutes of the fourth quarter.

The gate was still closed and Natchez contained, so AJ made the executive decision to follow Jace and Travis.

Eyes adjusting to the dark, she picked up speed and called her stepbrother. "Jace, the police are on the way. Stop now." She wove around the outside, forcing him to the right.

Good grief. Jace was incredibly fast for a man the size of a tank.

There was no way Travis could keep up with

him on his ankle. He'd only recently gotten the okay to remove the orthopedic boot.

She'd have to intercept Jace. Her only advantage was the fact that he didn't know Big Heart Ranch like she did. If she could just get him to run to the right, he'd fall into the shallow ravine and land in the dry creek bed and they'd have him.

"Whatever happened to plan A?" Travis asked, loud enough for her to hear.

"I'm improvising."

"Would have been good to know that before now."

Inching to Jace's outside was a lot like herding cows on a long-distance cattle drive. It helped to pretend her stepbrother was a recalcitrant steer. With each step, he got closer to the ravine. She kept moving back and forth, boxing him in.

AJ looked over her shoulder and so did Jace. Travis was right behind him. Jace had nowhere else to run.

Except at the last minute Jace stopped and turned. He snorted like a mad bull and, with his head down, he began to charge Travis. Jace wasn't trying to escape, he planned to mow down the man in his path.

"Jace," she called to distract him. He refused to budge from his trajectory.

Travis dodged, once. He dodged again, yet Jace

kept coming, a massive animal fueled by pent-up rage with a single-minded mission.

"Jace, stop!" she screamed.

The two men collided. Jace tucked himself beneath Travis, slamming him in the gut. Though Travis had crossed his arms in a protective gesture, the force tossed him in the air.

Jace rolled over, scrambled to his feet and ran in the opposite direction again. AJ prayed Travis was okay as she followed her stepbrother.

Once again, she was gaining on Jace, forcing him closer to the creek bed, until finally she heard him cry out as he stumbled into the ravine.

The ravine was steep and he'd never climb out without assistance. Mother Nature's jail cell for the cattle rustler.

She raced back to Travis, skidding to a halt on the grass beside him. He'd been knocked out cold.

"Travis," AJ murmured. She leaned over him and pushed a lock of hair from his forehead. His eyes were closed, the dark lashes spread on his pale face. His breathing was shallow.

AJ grabbed a fistful of his shirt and yelled in his ear. "Travis. Open your eyes, right this minute. Stop scaring me."

The rancher blinked as if trying to focus and shook his head. "Was that you screaming?"

"Yes." She sank to the ground next to him. Her

heart was about to burst with the realization that she loved this prideful, pigheaded man.

"Whoa." Travis grimaced and clutched his rib cage before he slowly sat up and glanced around. "Hey, are you okay?" he murmured, raising a hand and touching her hair.

AJ lifted her head. "Me? Yes. I'm fine. I'm wonderful."

"All I do is eat dust these days." He groaned and released a breath. "Help me up, will you."

She put her arm around him, feet planted apart, and struggled to get them both to their feet.

"Well, that was downright humiliating. I didn't even last eight seconds. Glad you were the only one around to witness it. I would have worn a Kevlar vest if I'd known I would be bull riding." He looked around. "Where's Jace? Please do not tell me that he got away."

"I sort of led him to the creek bed. He fell in the ravine."

"Nice job. Effective, yet perfectly legal." He straightened and groaned.

"What hurts?"

"What doesn't? I'm getting old," he muttered. "It doesn't help that he got me right in the same spot I bruised those ribs at the rodeo. This time he probably cracked a few. Knocked the wind right out of me."

"How's your ankle?"

"Oh, who knows? I'm falling apart."

"I'm so sorry."

"What are you sorry about? You were great. I had no idea you could run like that. I'm thinking next year we start a Big Heart Ranch softball team. Unless you'd prefer football."

She tried not to laugh. This was not a funny situation, she reminded herself. Yet she couldn't help smiling.

The sound of sirens once again broke through the spring night.

Jace was still in the ravine, moaning, when Chief Daniels approached and stood over him with a flashlight. "That's a sorry sight. You should be ashamed of yourself, son. Lem doesn't deserve this humiliation."

The deputy moved in and pulled Jace up. "Let's go, McAlester." The cowboy-turned-cattle-rustler protested loudly as he was being handcuffed and led to the back of the police vehicle.

"Travis, I'm going to have to start charging you for fuel," Chief Daniels said as he approached them.

"Oh, come on, Chief, I'm making you look good."

"That's one way to look at it." He narrowed his gaze and assessed Travis. "How many pieces are you in? Should I call an ambulance?"

"No, but thanks, I can get there on my own if need be."

"He cut the fence?" the chief continued.

"Yeah," Travis said. "We have the cutters and everything is on the video." He pointed to the cameras.

"Remember, cameras film everything. There isn't anything on there you don't want me to see, is there?"

"No, Chief, it's all good," Travis said.

"Then that video will be mighty handy when you have your day in court." He paused. "You are pressing charges this time, right?"

"Unfortunately, I am. Trespassing, property damage, jaywalking, littering and anything else you can think of." He looked over at AJ. "That all right with you?"

"Yes. I'll talk to Lem and see if we can get the pastor over to the jail for counseling."

Tripp and Dutch pulled up in the pickup truck. "Everything under control?" Dutch asked as he jumped out.

"Control, no," Travis said. "However, AJ managed to catch the cattle rustler and saved my life."

Tripp gave her a thumbs-up.

"Can you get Travis into your truck?" AJ asked. "He needs to go to the emergency room in Pawhuska."

Travis held up a hand. "The Timber urgent care will be fine."

AJ blinked. "Are you sure?"

"It's time I started admitting that I'm an old, broke-down bronc rider with a pretty face."

Dutch laughed. "Yeah, well, the good news is you aren't the oldest one on this ranch, you aren't the most broke-down and you sure ain't the prettiest."

AJ bit her lip at the truth in the words while Tripp and Dutch moved to either side of Travis and helped him to the truck.

When they left, she pulled nylon cable ties from her truck and secured Natchez's gate.

What was Lem going to do? She didn't know, but she was not going back to McAlester Ranch. Travis was wrong; she was ready to leave those memories in the past. She was ready for her future.

All she had to do was to make it through the grant inspection. Then she could decide what that path looked like. Decision-making time was coming again.

Decisions that were going to hurt.

Oh, how she longed for the comfort of her horse right now. She'd whisper in his ear and lay her head against his neck. And, for a few minutes, everything would be okay.

Her nose twitched as she fought against tears and stirred up some serious self-talk instead.

There's no time for sentiment. It's time to move on.

The pep talk wasn't helping. Already her chest was heavy with an unspoken ache. Yes, she was going to miss this place. After three months she'd memorized each ridge, hill and gopher hole on Big Heart Ranch.

She picked up a handful of red dirt and let it slip through her fingers. This was what mattered. The land. The land always told the truth.

She'd be thinking about Big Heart Ranch long after she'd moved on to her next job. And at night she'd lay awake and dare to think about Travis Maxwell.

Travis straightened his bolo tie and rubbed his solitary tooled-leather Justin boot on the back of his Wranglers until the toe shined. His other foot wore an orthopedic boot yet again.

He slipped his fingers between the blinds and peeked out the window of the conference room in the administrative building of Big Heart Ranch for the tenth time in as many minutes.

No AJ. This did not bode well.

The representative from the grant committee hadn't showed up, either, so he tried to remain positive.

Had AJ quit? Would she be a no-show today?

No, never. She'd promised and AJ Rowe didn't break promises. If he'd learned anything in the last ninety days, it was that she was a woman of character and his biggest failing was not exactly what she feared. He'd let her down. Not the other way around.

The torrent of misery he'd experienced the last few days was completely his own doing.

He rubbed his hands together and paced the floor. She'd show, he reminded himself again, but he wouldn't blame her if she'd had enough of this job and had taken off for greener pastures.

Truth was, he hadn't actually seen much of her in the last few days, though he'd heard plenty from everyone else about how she'd been slamming through the ranch like a tornado with a flight plan.

He'd seen evidence of that himself. The few times that they'd passed each other at the ranch, it seemed that she was going ninety-to-nothing in an effort to make sure a ranch in the middle of five hundred acres of red dirt was spit-shined, like a mother-in-law was due for a white-glove visit.

His cell phone vibrated and he looked at the text. Another dead end in his search for Gus. Eight days. The horse could be in another state by now. Or worse. Dread plagued him as well as visions of a slaughterhouse ending for AJ's animal.

Jace denied he'd sold Gus when Chief Daniels had questioned him. Flat-out lied. Par for the course.

Travis had to find Gus. AJ had lost everything. He knew what it was like to have everything plucked from you and was determined to help her salvage this small piece of herself.

The front door of the building whooshed open and he heard the tap-tap-tap of heels on the vinyl floor echo down the hall before AJ rushed into the room. She wore her gray interview suit, the same one she was wearing when they'd first met. Even her hair was pulled up in the same fancy twist like it was that day.

He couldn't resist a small smile. If only he could turn back the clock to that day. Ninety days later and he'd sure learned a lot. He'd learned that while he understood pain and suffering and loss, he didn't know diddly about women.

Basically he remained clueless.

If he'd simply admitted that in April, things might have gone easier for him.

AJ blew into the room and glanced around. "Sorry I'm late. I couldn't find my heels. I never wear heels. They were under the bunk." She kept babbling, her voice getting higher and tighter. "Ranger chewed my left shoe and I had to borrow heels from Tanya."

"We're fine," he soothed with a glance at his watch. "Don't stress."

"How's your ankle?" she asked.

"Had another checkup today with my regular doctor." Travis smiled. "I'm officially rodeo retired. He said, in no uncertain terms, no more bulls, broncs or cattle rustlers. If I agreed to the terms of probation, I can get this off again in another week." He gestured to his left foot.

"Wonderful." She swayed for a moment and sank into a chair, dropping her briefcase to the floor where it fell over with a thud. Her face crumpled.

Travis crossed the room. "AJ, what's wrong?"

"What if we don't pass?" Her voice trembled with panic.

He sat next to her, took her chilled hands in his and looked right into her eyes. She didn't pull away, which he took as a good sign.

"We're going to pass, don't worry. You've done everything to ensure that we'll pass."

"It will be all my fault if we don't. I take complete responsibility." Her shoulders sagged and her chin touched her chest in defeat.

This was what he'd done.

Travis sighed. The woman had single-handedly whipped his ranch into shape and with a few harsh and demeaning words he'd undermined her confidence.

"Listen to me." He put a finger beneath her chin and raised her face. "You, AJ Rowe, are the best assistant ranch foreman in the history of assistant ranch foremen. Anyone who says any different is plain wrong. Including me."

Her lower lip quivered and she nodded.

"Things have been a little rough for all of us lately, but we're going to get through this."

Lucy's admin, Iris, stepped into the room. She glanced at AJ and flinched. "Oh, excuse me."

"It's okay, Iris," Travis said.

"I'm sorry, but Ms. Williams is here from the Ranchers and Farmers Grant Committee."

AJ perked up and she wiped her fingers beneath her eyes. "Jackie Williams?"

"Yes, that's what she said."

"Do you know her?" Travis asked AJ.

"She was one of my professors at OU."

He raised his brows and offered a nod. "If this goes well, I may change my collegiate allegiance."

AJ stood and straightened her suit. "If this goes well, I'll make you."

Travis chuckled. AJ Rowe was back and handing out sass. "Of course, you will," he murmured.

She turned to Travis. "How do I look?"

As beautiful as the first time I met you. "Good. You look real good."

"Iris, you can bring her in," Travis said.

Moments later Jackie Williams entered the room and grinned. A friendly woman with a big smile, she walked straight to AJ and embraced her.

"AJ. I've wondered what happened to my most promising ranch student. I couldn't believe it when your paperwork came in. In fact, I specifically asked to do the walk-through at Big Heart Ranch."

"Oh, Jackie. Thank you so much." She turned to Travis. "Jackie, this is my supervisor, Big Heart Ranch foreman, Travis Maxwell."

Jackie cocked her head and pointed a finger in his direction. "Weren't you on the cover of *Tulsa Now* magazine?"

He held back a groan. "Yes, ma'am. I hope you won't hold that against me. My sisters made me do it. Wasn't my idea."

Jackie chuckled and held out a hand that Travis took. "Relax," she said. "The fact that you're Bachelor of the Year has no relevance to your application for the grant. Although I may ask for your autograph before I leave. For the girls in my office, you understand." She winked.

"Yes, ma'am."

"The information I read in the application is what is pertinent to today's visit." She turned to AJ. "Bison. I'm so impressed. Your ranch will be only the third ranch in the entire state to raise bison. You're pioneers."

AJ turned to Travis. "Pioneers. I like that."

Travis kept his mouth shut. Clearly he was outnumbered when it came to his uncharitable thoughts about bison.

"What made you decide to include bison?" Jackie asked.

"Biodiversity," Travis said with a nod. He was a little surprised he'd remembered the term, but there it was on the tip of his tongue when he needed it.

"Have you had any issues with the bison?"

Travis smiled and glanced at AJ. "Nope. No issues." And that was the truth. There were plenty of people issues, but the bison had been on good behavior.

He cleared his throat. "Everything's working smoothly. We like to think that we're fostering them. In return we're learning more about the environment. We're studying the forb and grasses in an effort to maintain a resilient and varied grazing pasture."

AJ's eyes widened and her jaw sagged.

"That's impressive. I like an open-minded rancher who stays on top of what's going on in the Ag industry."

"That's our Travis," AJ said.

"Shall we begin?" Jackie asked. She pulled a clipboard from her briefcase and glanced down at the boxes. "I'll want to tour all permanent fixtures for your livestock, and your yards and pastures. Then we can interview staff."

"Yes, ma'am," Travis said.

"Did you drive here from OK City?" AJ asked.

"I did. It was a beautiful drive this time of year, too. I plan to visit the Tall Grass Prairie Preserve when I leave here." She turned to AJ. "Why don't you and I do lunch first and catch up?"

"I'd really like that," AJ said. "The Oklahoma Rose in town has local beef. Travis tells me it's a fine establishment."

"Travis, would you care to join us?" Jackie asked.

"Oh, no, ma'am. You know what they say, never get between two women jawing about life or an old boyfriend."

Jackie stared at him and then burst out laughing. "Oh, that's good. I've never heard that one before." She turned to AJ and leaned close. "I like him."

"Stand in line. He's got quite the fan club," AJ murmured.

"Oh, I'll bet he does."

"This way, ladies," Travis said with a hand toward the hall. "I've got the bigger Ute parked outside. It'll fit all of us."

Travis worked to remain calm as he followed the chatting women down the hall. He tugged at the collar of his dress shirt.

Ninety days and five years of his life. His entire career was on the line in this walk-through that would take all of an hour or two, give or take.

Yet deep inside he sensed a release, as if the

Lord was telling him to let it go. He'd already messed up once this week. He didn't intend to do it again. Travis took a deep breath and let go, entrusting everything to AJ and Him.

And why not? He glanced at AJ. She was standing tall, her confidence back in place, grinning like everything was going to be all right. Somehow, though the tables had turned and he was the one with the case of the jitters now, he believed her. One way or another, everything was going to be all right.

Chapter Twelve

"I need your help," Travis said.

Tripp looked up from the mare he was grooming and pushed his hat to the back of his head. "How's that?"

"I have to track down a horse. Any idea how to do that?"

"Is this a trick question?" he asked as he brushed the horse's copper flank.

"Look, I've exhausted all the usual options. I didn't think it was going to be this difficult or I would have come to you first."

"What's going on, Travis?"

"AJ's horse is missing."

Tripp's hand stopped its movement. "I didn't know she had a horse."

"She does. Gus. At least, she had a horse, eight days ago."

"How'd you find that out?"

"Something AJ said struck me as off when we were sort of talking. So I called her stepfather after we arrested Jace. Turns out Jace found Gus's papers and sold him."

"Nothing illegal about that."

"He didn't own the horse and denies selling the horse. So it's Lem's word against his." He released a breath of frustration. "I've been calling around myself, but haven't made any traction."

"So AJ's talking to you? Does she know you're looking for her horse?"

"We're making headway. But no, she doesn't know. I don't want to get her hopes up yet."

"I've got a few favors I can pull in."

"Great. Thanks." He turned to go.

"Hold it," Tripp said.

Travis looked back. "I knew that was way too easy."

"My laptop is five years old and it was used when Lucy gave it to me. They laugh when I call for tech support."

"Fine. I'll order you a new one."

Tripp gave a nod of thanks.

"Anything else?"

"I'm a simple man with simple needs. But since you mentioned it, my desk chair is plum worn out. I'm practically sitting on the ground."

"Simple man, my foot," Travis muttered as he headed out of the stable and to his truck.

When his cell phone rang later, he recognized Tripp's number. "You found Gus?"

"Don't sound so hopeful. I talked to Lem McAlester myself and the horse was most likely taken to a kill buyer. They buy the horses cheap and sell them to a slaughterhouse."

"That's what I was afraid of." A prickle of dread clutched Travis. Everyone had let AJ down and she kept on giving. She didn't deserve this and he'd do everything he could to save Gus for her.

"Travis, you there?" Tripp asked.

"Yeah. I'm here. Where's this kill buyer located?"

"Closer than you want to know. My contact says the guy running the operation hasn't made a shipment yet this month, so the horse is most likely still there."

"Eight days. I'm afraid to think about the kind of shape that horse might be in by now."

Tripp nodded. "Yep. Me, too."

"Do you have an address?"

"I do. Are you ready to head out there?"

"Yeah. Can you hook up the trailer to the ranch dually for me?"

"Yep."

"I need to get cash at the bank. Grab Dutch and I'll meet you both in the parking lot in an hour."

"Let's do this," Tripp said as they got into the Silverado sixty minutes later. He adjusted his seat belt and began to back the trailer up enough to allow him to circle out the ranch drive.

"How far is this place?" Dutch asked from the rear seat of the cab.

"Twenty minutes outside Timber."

"So close?" Travis returned. "Right in our backyard all this time. Sort of makes me sick to think about it."

Tripp nodded. "I called Chief Daniels. Once we're out of there and Gus is safe, he's going to raid the place. Any horse without papers will be removed."

"We can't save them all," Travis said, "but it's a start."

Dutch stuck his head up front from the back seat of the cab. "I don't want to rub salt in your wounds or nothing, but have you talked to AJ again, boss? I mean like we discussed."

"We have a tenuous relationship, at best. As long as it's about business, we're good."

"Can't say I blame her," Dutch murmured.

"Hey, whose side are you on?"

Dutch shrugged. "Sometimes the only one you can trust is your horse."

"How is it Rue puts up with you?" Travis asked.

"My charm, probably."

"Aren't you going to help me out here?" Travis said to Tripp.

"I don't see as I can. You got yourself into this mess."

"Okay, look, I'll admit it," Travis said. "I've hit an all-time low. I thought I was low when I was arm candy for a rich buckle bunny. But here I met someone who doesn't care about the outside, who apparently accepted me as I am all along, and I totally let her down."

"That's an understatement," Dutch muttered. "I'll never see another pie thanks to you."

"I messed up. I apologized." He raised his palms. "What more can I do?"

"You have to keep going after her until she gets tired of seeing your face and forgives you," Dutch said. "Go after her, cowboy."

"That's your advice?" Travis looked at him and rolled his eyes. "That's the best you got?"

"When was the last time you wooed a woman?" Tripp asked.

"Too long," Travis admitted.

"All right. Then listen to the man. Dutch knows what he's talking about. You don't get to be his age without learning something."

"That's somehow not reassuring. I heard tell that Dutch gets all his advice from watching John Wayne movies."

"Did you just insult me?" Dutch asked.

Travis was saved from answering when Tripp

turned the truck into a long drive with a metal gate barring the entrance.

"Will you look at that barn? A strong wind comes by and it'll be a pile of kindling," Dutch said. "The place ought to be condemned."

Tripp hit the horn until an old-timer came out and opened the gate.

"Come on, Dutch. Let's go," Travis said. "Let me do the talking."

"Not sure that's your best idea today," Dutch mumbled.

Travis glared at him as he jumped down from the Silverado.

"Not so fast there, mister," the wrangler at the gate said. He pulled his battered Stetson down and pointed his shotgun at them. "Stay right by your vehicle. Both of you. I may be old, but I hold all the cards. And I don't like trespassers."

Travis raised both hands. "Yes, sir. We're here to buy a horse. Not looking for trouble."

"Glad to hear that. What sort of horse? We've got all kinds."

"Blue roan gelding. White stockings. Around seventeen years old."

"You're interested in that geriatric?"

"It's for my grandmother. She likes geriatrics."

The old cowboy shook his head, spit his chaw on the ground and leaned against the fence.

"How bad does your grandmother want this particular horse?"

"She's willing to pay."

"Cash."

Travis nodded. "Granny understands."

When the cowboy named his price, Travis's jaw sagged. "That's a little outside my grandmother's budget."

"Then buy her a cat."

"Okay. Okay." Travis gestured to his wallet. "I'll take the horse."

"And I'll take your money."

"Deal."

The cowboy offered a toothless grin and turned toward the dilapidated barn structure with its sagging roof and little hope of sunlight.

Tripp stuck his head out the window when the old man was out of earshot. "Are you out of your ever-loving mind?"

"Yes," Travis said. "I am."

"Remind me never to fall in love," Tripp returned. "I can't afford the price tag."

Dutch snorted at the words.

When Gus was led out of the dark barn, with a dirty rope around his neck, Travis released the breath he'd been holding. He handed over an envelope of cash in exchange for the rope. When the gate was opened, he quickly led Gus to the trailer.

"It's okay, boy. We're going home to AJ." He

rubbed a hand over the horse's flank with an assessing eye for injuries.

"How long did you say he's been in that place?" Dutch asked as he shook his head and clucked his tongue.

"Eight days."

"Looks dehydrated," Dutch said. "And he's got some sores on his legs. I'll phone ahead for the vet to meet us at the ranch."

"Yeah, I'd like to do more than arrest those guys." Travis banged a hand on the truck door. "Start the truck, Tripp. We're getting out of here before they change their mind."

Dutch closed the metal door of the trailer and nodded to Travis. They hopped into the cab of the truck.

"Let's go," Travis said.

"Chief Daniels just texted me," Tripp said. "He and his deputy are waiting for us to leave. They've got the Oklahoma Highway Patrol with them and they have a search warrant."

"Good," Travis returned.

"He also wants to know if we've considered a career in law enforcement."

"What?" Travis's head swiveled toward Tripp.

"Yeah. Says his two-man force can hardly keep up with all the offenders we keep tossing his way."

Travis pointed a finger in the air as the sound of wailing sirens echoed, getting closer and closer.

"Hear that?" Tripp asked.

"I do. Best sound I've heard in a long time," Travis said.

"Where we going to take Gus?" Dutch asked.

"Let's head up to the girls' ranch equestrian center for now and have the vet examine him there." He turned to Tripp. "That work for you?"

Tripp nodded. "When are you going to tell AJ we found him?"

AJ. All he really wanted was to ease her pain. Travis said a silent prayer that Gus would be okay.

"After the vet checks him out," he replied.

"Best be soon," Dutch said. "Before she finds a better job."

"I guess I better drive fast then," Tripp muttered.

"I expect grief from Dutch," Travis said. "But you?" He stared at Tripp. "I really liked you better when you didn't talk so much."

"I only talk when I have something to say. Thanks to your love life, I may talk for days. Get used to it."

"Great. Just great."

"Mind if I ask where you got all that cash?" Tripp continued.

"Took it out of the bank. I've been saving for a truck."

"Your Raptor fund?" Tripp's face registered more emotion than he'd seen on the horse whisperer's face in a long time. "Why would you do that?"

"You know why. This cowboy is in love. That's why," Dutch said with a snort.

Travis couldn't help a smile. He wasn't totally opposed to the idea of being in love. Though he knew at this point it was a real long shot that AJ would forgive him. He settled back in the seat. "I did it because I'd rather have a horse than a truck."

And he'd rather see the look on AJ's face when she saw Gus than drive a fancy pickup truck around town all by himself. It might not change things between them, but at least he'd have peace of mind knowing she wasn't crying herself to sleep at night anymore. That was the only thing he could be sure of right now. And he was good with it.

"Aren't you going in?" Lucy Maxwell Harris asked.

AJ turned at the friendly voice. "Oh, yes. Of course." The chow hall door had been propped open for the staff appreciation party and she entered with two of her blackberry pies stacked in carriers in her hands.

"Your famous pie," Lucy said as they walked down into the cafeteria together.

"My pies are famous?"

"Yes, according to the ranch scuttlebutt. Of

course, I've never tasted them. Something I plan to remedy tonight."

AJ smiled and glanced over at the white pastry box tied with string that dangled from Lucy's fingers. "What did you bring?"

"Gourmet cookies. I didn't make them. Turning on the oven nauseates me. Don't ask me why. My physician is baffled. I've never been pregnant before, so I don't understand, either." She offered a conspiratorial smile. "I got these cookies from a well-known shop in Pawhuska. They're amazing. So delicious, that the first dozen I purchased were confiscated by my family. I had to send Jack back to Pawhuska a second time. I feel certain that I'll be forgiven for bringing store-bought treats."

"I already forgive you."

Lucy wrapped an arm around AJ. "Aren't you just so excited that we get to announce the grant approval at the party?"

AJ stumbled and nearly dropped the pies. Travis wasn't even around and he managed to tangle her feet and her thoughts long-distance.

"Careful," Lucy said.

"What did you say about the grant?" AJ asked.

"You were approved."

"I didn't realize."

"Travis didn't tell you?" Lucy frowned. "I guess he wanted it to be a surprise."

"Oh, I'm surprised." She slowly shook her head. "So the grant was approved."

"AJ, are you all right?" Lucy placed a gentle hand on AJ's arm. "I've heard that things between you and my brother have been strained. And trust me, I wanted to interfere. It took every bit of restraint not to."

"That's over. We're fine. No worries."

"Are you sure?"

"Yes. Absolutely. A little livestock conflict of interest." And things were for certain over between her and Travis, she mentally added.

"Okay, I'll catch you later, then. Come and find me."

AJ stood at the outside edge of the room as friendly faces mingled in the large cafeteria, greeting each other. She recognized nearly everyone and it was like a big family party, exactly as Rue had said.

Delicious aromas wove through the air, begging her to peek at the buffet table. Crock-Pots lined one table, salads and side dishes another, while desserts overflowed three tables. This crew had a serious sweet tooth.

Yet, as the party swirled around her, AJ's steps faltered. What was the point in joining in this welcoming family event when she would be leaving soon?

"Isn't this fun?" Rue said as she sidled next to AJ.

"Fun. Yes." AJ nodded, working hard to be enthusiastic when all she really felt was dread crushing her.

"Dear, are you all right?" Rue asked.

"You're the second person to ask me that. I must look really bad."

"No. You look exhausted."

"I am tired. It's been an excruciatingly long week."

"That long, huh? Well, I heard from Dutch that you've spent nearly every night in your truck. He also told me that you stopped a rustler and saved Travis's life." She turned to AJ. "That was a direct quote."

"Dutch has a vivid imagination, doesn't he?"

"He's still doing marathon Western movies. In his eyes, you're pretty much Dale Evans." She turned to AJ. "If you could sing 'Happy Trails,' that would make his day."

AJ laughed, her mood lightening. "I have many talents, however singing is not one of them. Although, 'Happy Trails' seems an appropriate theme song for my life at the moment."

"It's actually a relief to know you aren't perfect." Rue reached for the pies in AJ's hands. "Let me take those. I'll put them on the table."

"Thank you, Rue."

"Oh, and did you see what Tripp brought?"

"Tripp? No, I didn't."

"Spinach lasagna roll-ups. They're in a delicate tomato sauce." She winked. "Yes. I cheated and sampled."

"No beef?"

"Tripp is a vegetarian."

"A vegetarian who works on a cattle ranch. Makes perfect sense."

"In his defense, there wasn't a single bovine or even a chicken on Big Heart Ranch when he started with us back in the day." Rue smiled and gestured to the pies. "I'll be right back."

Across the room, Emma flitted from one guest to the next. She spotted AJ and waved. AJ waved back. Who didn't love Emma? Why couldn't she be more like Emma Maxwell?

Charming and adorable, instead of socially awkward with an acerbic wit. A widow with two babies, Emma juggled everything and selflessly put everyone before herself. She was never without a kind word.

Regret pierced her and belatedly she wished she'd spent more time with Emma instead of hiding in the bunkhouse. It was far too late to remedy that now. She'd be gone soon. Big Heart Ranch would be just a memory.

Lucy moved through the crowd, exchanging pleasantries, until she stood at the front of the room with a small microphone in her hand. She tapped it with a knuckle to get everyone's attention.

"First, I want to thank the entire staff for being here. Before we eat, I've asked Pastor Parr to say a prayer for our summer ahead and to bless our meal."

Head bowed, AJ tried to focus on the prayer but her mind kept whirling as she tried to imagine life without the friends of Big Heart Ranch.

"Amen."

A sober and thankful chorus of amens echoed across the room before Lucy took the microphone again.

"The next item on tonight's agenda is good news that I'll let my brother share with you."

The rustle of people turning could be heard as everyone looked around the room.

"Travis?"

Lucy's gaze scanned the cafeteria. "Travis?" she repeated.

Staff followed her lead and turned to look for the Maxwell sibling.

Travis came jogging up to the front a moment later with a smile in place. "Sorry. You know how it is. Another fire to put out." He took the mic from his sister and gave her a kiss on her cheek.

"The good news is that the Emerging Ranch Grant was approved unanimously by the committee. This means we are well on our way to a self-sustaining beef production program that will feed the families and staff of Big Heart Ranch and provide educational and funding opportunities for the future. We have our assistant foreman AJ Rowe and her team to thank for that."

The room exploded with applause and AJ found herself surrounded by well-wishers heaping words of appreciation and praise on her. Her hand was pumped with congratulatory handshakes and she was wrapped in hugs and air-kissed.

Overwhelmed, she slipped to the back of the room as the buffet line began.

"Aren't you eating?" Tripp asked, stepping up beside her.

"Are you really a chef?" She glanced up at the tall cowboy.

He offered a slow smile. "I can cook."

"I might try your spinach lasagna roll-ups."

"And I might try your pie."

"You might. If there's any left."

Tripp chuckled and headed to the dessert table.

Okay, she'd try Tripp's lasagna before she returned to the bunkhouse. If not, she might spend the rest of her life pondering the urban legend about the horse whisperer who may or may not have been a famous chef hiding on Big Heart Ranch.

"Tripp's lasagna?" Dutch asked as she settled into a chair at one of the cafeteria-style tables.

She nodded, took a bite and then looked down at the plate. "How did he do that?"

"Do what?"

"I see nothing unusual on this plate. Do you?" She moved the food gently with her fork. "Yet my mouth just told me that something amazing landed on my tongue and it wants more. Demanded more. Immediately."

"Yeah, that's our Tripp." He gave a nod of understanding.

"I'm stunned."

"You need a beverage," Dutch said.

"No. Absolutely not. I want this to linger on my lips as long as possible."

"You're an odd duck, AJ. I like you, but you're an odd one."

"Thank you, Dutch. I like you, too."

"You talk to Travis?" he asked as he examined the fare on his plate.

"No? Why?"

"Just asking." He bobbed up and down and from side to side, attempting to see around people in an effort to glimpse the dessert table. "You brought pie!"

Dutch didn't wait for a response but race-walked across the room.

When Lucy and Emma began walking around the room, handing out gift bags and smiles, AJ looked around for their brother. Where was Travis? From the corner of her eye she saw him crossing the room to her. Standing, she left both her dinner and the gift bag and stepped into the hall.

Not fast enough apparently. She heard footsteps behind her.

"Seriously? You left Tripp's lasagna?"

Travis was at her side in a heartbeat. He held out the plate of food and the gift bag she'd abandoned.

"Thank you," she said, accepting both.

"Where are you going?" he asked. "Anywhere in particular or just as far away from me as possible?"

"Don't be dramatic. I'm going to get a good night's sleep. Three hours a night isn't cutting it." Honestly, she was tired.

"After that?" He continued to walk next to her, his stride slowing.

"I'm leaving, Travis. I did what I said I would do. My commitment to the ranch has been fulfilled."

He blocked her way, his jaw tight. "We got the grant. Didn't you hear that part?"

"No, *you* got the grant. It's all about you, Travis. You, who never even let me know it was approved. What was I? Collateral damage on the way to you getting what you wanted?"

"That couldn't be further from the truth."

"Try to see things from where I stand," she said. "You didn't hesitate for one moment to let me know it was my fault when those bison were loose. Yet you never even had the courtesy to tell me when the grant was approved."

"It wasn't like that, AJ." He ran a hand through his hair. "I was tied up this afternoon and I didn't find out the grant was approved until right before the party. I told Lucy and…well, you know my sister. As usual, she ran with it, like a runaway horse."

"I should have been the first person you told. I deserved that much. But you told Lucy because you need her approval." She sighed. "What you don't get is that you don't need her approval. Lucy already believes in you."

AJ shrugged. "It doesn't matter. This is a no-win situation for me." She swallowed but couldn't stop the words welling up. "I'll always be the fall girl when things go wrong at Big Heart Ranch. If you could only let go," she mused. "Believe in yourself. Believe in me."

"That's not true. It might have been true once." Travis took a deep breath. "Okay, it was true up until the grant walk-through. But it's not anymore. You taught me to let go, AJ. You and the big guy." He shook his head when she didn't say anything.

"I guess if your heart is set on leaving, there's nothing I can do."

Her heart? What her heart was set on was breaking.

"I don't know what to tell you, Travis. I'm so confused. I couldn't stand to ever have you look at me the way you did when you thought I was responsible for the bison getting loose. Thinking I disappointed you nearly did me in."

"I was wrong then, AJ. I want you to stay on more than anything, because you're the only person who can do the job." He paused and met her gaze. "I was wrong tonight. I should have told you first. You deserved that. You earned that. Can you think about giving me a second chance to get something right?"

She stared at him. "Something right?"

He took the bag and the plate from her hands and walked to the Ute and placed them in the back. "Come with me."

"Where? Where am I going?"

"Trust me one last time, AJ. Please?"

A long, uncomfortable silence stretched between them.

Exhaustion dogged her steps when all she really wanted was for this day to end. The set of Travis's jaw said that he wasn't going to leave until she gave in.

"Okay, Travis. Okay," she murmured.

She slid into the Ute and he started the engine. They drove the perimeter of Big Heart Ranch silently until they reached the girls' ranch equestrian center. Travis parked the vehicle and nodded toward the open doors. Though it was after hours, all the lights were on.

"The stable?"

He nodded.

Goose bumps danced down her arms as she followed him, their footsteps echoing on the plank flooring. The building was silent, except for the quiet shuffling of horses. Occasionally a snuffle or snort could be heard as she passed a stall. Travis stopped at a stall on the very end.

The ranch's vet blocked the entrance to this particular stall.

"Doc?" Travis called.

The vet turned and smiled. "He's going to be fine. I'll keep a close eye on him and we'll continue the IVs until he's sufficiently hydrated. I've left dressing change instructions with Tripp."

"What's going on?" AJ murmured.

The vet stepped aside and she stared at the horse in the stall. "Gus," she breathed, her thoughts bouncing from disbelief to stunned surprise. She stepped into the small space covered with fresh hay and stumbled, her knees nearly buckling.

Travis reached out a hand to steady her.

"Oh, Gus. You came back to me." AJ wrapped her arms around the gelding.

Gus nickered and turned his nose into AJ to offer an affectionate nuzzle. His big, round, chocolate eyes flickered with recognition.

"I thought I lost you, too, buddy." AJ tucked her head into the animal's neck and wept silently.

A hand touched her shoulder. "Are you going to be okay?"

Travis.

AJ sniffed and wiped her eyes before she turned to face him. The vet quietly waited outside in the doorway of the stable.

"How did you find him?"

"Tripp located Gus. Once he did the legwork, we grabbed Dutch and picked him up."

"That simple?"

"Maybe not quite that simple. He's here and he's going to be fine. That's what matters, right?"

She ran a hand over the horse's coat, examining him. "How are his legs?" she asked, inspecting the gauze bandages.

"He's got a few sores but Doc has everything under control. We've got the supplies and salve for dressing changes. The dehydration was the biggest concern. He's over that hump now. Really perked up once he saw you. You're the best medicine this horse could have."

"Oh, Travis. I don't know how to thank you."

"You just did. It's all good."

She met his dark eyes and they were tinged with sadness. "But—"

He raised a hand and held out the Ute keys. "I'll catch a ride back with the vet. Stay as long as you like."

"Thank you."

"You already said that."

"It seems insignificant."

When he left she let out a breath and said a silent prayer of thanksgiving. She put her arms over the stall gate and stared at Gus, watching the drip of the IV, grateful for this second chance with her horse.

"I see you found him," Tripp murmured.

She glanced up. "You knew and didn't say anything."

He shrugged. "Wasn't my place."

"Tell me what happened. I'm so confused. I can't put this behind me until I understand how you found him."

Tripp eyed her and frowned.

"I asked Travis and he won't elaborate. If you don't tell me, then I'll have to go ask Dutch. You know he'll tell me anything I want to know for blackberry pie."

"You'd do that?" Tripp clucked his tongue. "Here I thought you were a sweet girl."

"You have no idea what I am capable of."

He raised his brows. "Travis saved your horse from a short trip to the slaughterhouse."

A gasp slipped from her lips. "How? How did he do that?"

"That's where this story gets interesting. Seems he used his truck fund to negotiate Gus's release."

"His Raptor money?" AJ shoved her hair back over her shoulder.

"You know about that?"

"Yes," she murmured. "I know he's been saving for five years. The Raptor is his dream."

"A man doesn't share his dreams with just anyone, you know. And he doesn't forget his dreams for just anyone."

Tripp pushed off from the wall and walked out of the stable. His steps were slow and nearly silent as he left.

AJ's hand covered her mouth. She turned to Gus. "What are we going to do? Everything is all messed up. I don't even know where to start to untangle this mess."

Gus nudged her with his nose as if pushing her out of the stall to fix things.

"You're right. I'm going to get some sleep and then I'll find Travis when I can think clearly." AJ ran a hand over Gus's nose and kissed him. "Do you think he'll forgive me when I've been so unforgiving?"

Gus whinnied.

"I have to try," she whispered to her horse. "Because I realized something tonight. This is the end of the trail for us. Big Heart Ranch is our home and I've got to make things right."

Chapter Thirteen

Before the sun said hello, AJ slipped into the stable to check on Gus. The IV bag had been changed, as had his bandages. Apparently, Tripp rose even earlier than she did. Satisfied Gus was coming along, she returned to the bunkhouse.

She could pretend that it was just another day on Big Heart Ranch. Except it wasn't. What would today hold? Yesterday she was certain and now… now she could only pray for guidance.

From the kitchen window she could see a Ute pull up to the bunkhouse. Rue was behind the wheel. Ranger pawed at the door, excited to see the general.

"Morning, Rue," AJ said. She scooped up the pup, opened the screen and stepped outside.

"Is it true that you're leaving?"

"I'm not sure what my plans are."

"This is very worrisome. I don't understand

how two smart people can be so silly. Lucy and Emma are very concerned, but they promised Travis they'd mind their own business." She smiled. "Minding their own business is pure torture. They sent me here."

Dutch rode up on his horse. "How's Gus?"

"Improving. Thank you for rescuing him."

"Aw, it was all Travis." A blush crept up the cowboy's face.

"Just the same. I am very appreciative."

"Travis is in his office. I saw him go in about an hour ago after he rode the fences," Dutch said.

"You're telling me about Travis's schedule for informational purposes? Or did Lucy and Emma send you, too?"

"I'm telling you so you can get moving and take care of this situation that you and Travis have found yourselves flat in the middle of. You're each riding a stubborn mule going in the wrong direction and wondering why you can't see eye-to-eye."

AJ cocked her head and looked at him. "Was that from a movie?"

"No, ma'am. That was pure Dutch Stevens."

"I might start collecting Dutch-isms. Maybe write a book."

"You're joshing."

"No. I'm serious." She turned to Rue. "What do you think?"

"Splendid idea. We could sell them to the staff. Make a fortune for the ranch."

"See, Rue gets it." She smiled. "I'd like to talk to the vet this morning. Do you know when he's at the ranch?"

"He makes rounds in the afternoon," Dutch answered. "Go see Travis. You're wasting time."

"I've got nothing but time, Dutch."

"That's what you think." He snorted.

"I really appreciate your concern. I haven't had anyone care about me like this in a very long time, but you're forgetting one thing. I don't work here anymore. I'm not in any rush to do anything."

"You don't work here anymore? That can't be true," Dutch said. He scratched his head. "The new schedule just came out this morning and I saw your name on it. You're on call tonight and you have pasture maintenance this afternoon."

"No. That can't be correct. I told Travis last night."

"You better find out what's going on, dear," Rue said.

"You two are not going to leave me alone until I do. Are you?" She narrowed her eyes at Dutch and Rue. "Are you coming with me?"

"No. I reckon this is one dance we'll sit out," Dutch said. "Got any pie left?"

"No pie until I find out what's going on."

"Well, that ain't fair, after all this advocating I'm doing on your behalf."

"Advocating? That's what you call it?"

"Well, sure, and I might be persuaded to stay out of your hair for the rest of the day if I had pie."

"Okay, fine. The pie's hidden in the laundry room."

AJ walked toward Travis's office, her frustration moving her along at a fast clip. This might very well be the last time she'd make this early morning walk from the bunkhouse to his office. No more tidying up the paperwork. No more drinking endless pots of coffee with the boss.

No more Travis, her mind shot back. And hadn't she and Gus decided they'd wanted to stay? How was she going to turn things around and make sure Travis understood that they were a team? That together they had a future running the ranch. Certainly she longed for much more than that, but she had to have his trust before she'd ever have his heart.

The smell of horse sweat and hay was strong as she passed the stables where morning riding lessons had already begun.

"Hi, Miss AJ," one of the girls called. "Will you be helping us with Bess today?"

AJ waved. "I'll let you know."

Barrel racing lessons. She'd nearly forgotten. Big Heart Ranch held its own rodeo at the end of summer, and she'd offered to train two promising riding students.

Tripp stood in the door of the stables as she passed. He offered a nod of greeting.

"Did you try my pie?" she asked.

"Got it waiting for me in the refrigerator. You try my spinach lasagna roll-ups?"

"I did and my mouth refuses to eat mediocre food ever again." She smiled and kept moving toward the foreman's office.

Her steps slowed as she got closer yet, oddly enough, her heart picked up speed.

What was she going to say? She felt like she was playing checkers and a few pieces were missing. Where should she move? Forward? Backward? Give up?

She knocked and turned the handle on the door. From inside Travis growled.

"Good morning to you, too," she said.

Travis narrowed his eyes as she stepped into the room. He was seated at his desk, going through a stack of papers.

"What happened to this place?" AJ glanced around at the disorder.

"I needed the paperwork on Natchez and couldn't find it anywhere."

AJ walked over to the filing cabinet and fingered through the neat files. "N for Natchez. A little known coding system I use, called the alphabet." She pulled out a file and handed it to him.

"Thank you." Travis offered a grim smile. "Can I help you with something?"

"You spent your truck money on Gus," she blurted out.

He groaned. "Who told you that? Nobody on this ranch can keep their lips zipped. Have you noticed this?"

"Can we talk, please?" AJ asked.

"I don't see what there is to talk about. You've made yourself pretty clear. I don't want you to change your mind and stay because you feel guilty about me and the whole Gus issue."

"I don't feel guilty. I feel appreciative to have friends who care about me."

"Okay." He raised a brow. "Was there something else?"

"Dutch says I'm still on the schedule."

"You are."

"But I quit last night."

"I didn't see any letter of resignation, so technically you're still an employee."

"I haven't had a chance to write one up yet. But you understood my intention."

"Human resources doesn't care about intention. I need a letter." He frowned. "I told you, I won't hold you back if you don't want to be here. I'll provide a recommendation for your new job.

You write that letter and we'll get the ball rolling." Travis picked up his coffee and took a long swig.

"What if I don't want to get the ball rolling? What if I changed my mind?"

He began to sputter and choke.

"Are you all right?" AJ moved to his side.

Travis held up a palm. "What did you say?"

"I asked if you're all right."

"No. Before that."

"I said I've changed my mind. The truth is that I don't want to be anywhere but Big Heart Ranch. I've waited my entire life for this place. I just didn't know what I was searching for. I know now."

Travis reached for her hand. "Do you mean that?" His brown eyes searched her face.

"Yes. I'm sorry that I've made it impossible for you to be forgiven. And now here I am groveling and asking you to forgive me." She met his gaze.

"Why are you apologizing?"

"Yesterday afternoon you were rescuing my horse. That's why you didn't have time to tell me about the grant."

Travis shrugged. "I still should have told you before I told Lucy."

"I'm willing to do anything if you'll give me another chance."

"I thought that was my line," he said.

"I guess we're at an impasse."

"I think I can see to the other side of this, except I've got one small problem."

"Oh?"

"I'm pretty sure I'm in love with you, Amanda."

"What? You can't be in love with me."

"Why not?"

"I'm your assistant foreman."

"Could I fire you and tell you I love you and then rehire you?"

She burst out laughing. "That's the craziest thing I ever heard."

Travis stepped closer and slipped his arms around her waist. "You're fired." He settled his lips on hers for a long, lingering kiss.

"I may have to join your Swoon Society. That was a very nice kiss and your idea has merit, too."

If she wasn't an employee she was free to have coffee in the Timber Diner with Travis. Why, they could even have dinner at the Oklahoma Rose.

No, she nixed the idea. It was time to stop worrying about what anyone but the Lord had to say.

"I don't want to be fired," she announced.

"You don't?"

"No. I want to work at Big Heart Ranch and I want the world to know I'm crazy about the foreman."

"You're what?"

"I'm crazy in love with you, Travis Maxwell."

Travis closed his eyes and took a shaky breath before his lips touched hers again.

"You know, for a day that started out sort of sideways, things are really looking up," he murmured against her mouth.

"Are you saying this works for you?"

"Let's review to make sure I understand."

AJ nodded. "I forgive you. You forgive me."

"And you love me?" he said with wonder. "I thought I had to take it slow. You were barely getting used to friendship."

"That was before Jace knocked you out cold in the pasture. In that split second I realized that I thought Gus's disappearance meant I'd lost everything. I was wrong. I still had you and I don't want to ever lose you, Travis."

She laced her fingers with his. "The funny thing about forgiveness is that it's really more about you than it is about the other person."

"You're right."

"Do I have my job back?" she asked.

"You're my favorite assistant foreman and you're my friend. I don't want to lose you, AJ."

"You haven't. I'm here forever."

"That's a long time," he said.

"Yes. I'm counting on that."

AJ sat at the top of the ridge astride Gus, looking out over Big Heart Ranch. There was so much to be thankful for. Gus was back to his old self and so was she.

The summer program had begun and she fell into bed each night happy and exhausted. Ranger had flunked obedience school and she had no intention of enrolling him again. Yes, life was good.

She stared in the direction of McAlester Ranch. It was time to let it go. With Jace in jail, even for a short time, Lem had made the decision to pack up and move to Texas to live with his brother. Jace had put the ranch up for sale.

Travis had offered to buy McAlester Ranch but she'd turned down the idea. Resurrecting her father's ranch wouldn't bring her parents back. It was time to put down roots and she was happy to do that at Big Heart.

Her phone buzzed and she glanced at the screen. Travis was texting her.

Have you checked the bison this evening?

I'm not assigned to evening check. Is there a problem?

Could be.

She typed a response.

What does that mean?

Have you been over to the bison pasture lately?

No, I was checking on the weaned calves before heading in for dinner.

I'd get over there if I were you.

AJ was afraid to answer. She slipped her phone into her pocket and groaned. Not now. Not when things were going so good.

She nudged her horse around. "Come on, Gus. Let's go see what kind of trouble those bison got us into this time." Together they galloped over the ridge and around the pond to the north pasture. As the bison paddock came into view, she eased up on the reins. "Whoa, boy." She patted Gus's neck and stared out at the big animals.

"What...?" AJ blinked. There were three bison in the pasture instead of two. She glanced around, looking for Travis, but saw nothing. He would be furious. He still couldn't stand the animals, though he now grudgingly admitted they had helped with the grant. His nicknames for them were Bio and Diva. She chuckled. He'd gotten that from biodiversity.

Inching closer, it appeared there were sandwich board signs draped over the bison like saddlebags.

Words were on the signs in big red letters.

"'Amanda Rowe,'" she murmured, reading the

first sign. Her gaze moved to the second sign. "'Marry me?'" Her eyes rounded and she began to tremble as she looked to the third sign. "'Will you.'"

"Aw, really?" Travis growled. He came up behind her on Midnight. "I tell you, those bison are nothing but trouble."

AJ whirled around in the saddle. "Travis? What's going on?"

He slid from his horse and stomped to the fence. Unlocking the padlock gate, he went in and pushed the bison cows around, rearranging their order until the signs read "Amanda Rowe. Will you marry me?"

She opened her mouth and stared.

Locking the gate behind him, he approached her horse. "That's better." A huge grin was on his face.

"There are three bison in there," she said.

"That's all you noticed?"

"I'm just saying."

"I picked one up at a special sale this morning. Dutch went with me. I figured we can manage three, for educational purposes. We don't have enough grazing land for more."

"Three bison cows, correct?"

"I'm a rancher. I get how that works. Yes, all three are female." He frowned. "Seriously, is that all you noticed?" He glanced back at the signs. "Are the words too small to read? Try moving closer."

She slipped her leg over the saddle and slid from Gus to the ground. "Why did you buy another bison? I thought you hate bison."

"Your birthday is tomorrow. I figured another would make you happy."

AJ wiped at the moisture in her eyes. "I'm already happy."

"Whoa!" Concern flashed across his face and he pulled her into his arms. "You don't look happy. Are you crying?"

"No. I don't cry. It's very dusty out here."

"Right."

"Remember when you asked me what I dream of?" she whispered against his shoulder.

"Yeah. As I recall you said something about how you don't dream."

"Something happened that day in Pawnee. Something changed. I began to dream of a home. About a place I could put down roots, unpack my boxes and never leave. I dreamed of horses, cows and children, along with my house. My own children." She bit her lip.

"I don't suppose I'm anywhere in those dreams," he whispered against her hair.

AJ stepped back from the circle of his arms and met his gaze. She trembled beneath his tender scrutiny. "You started those dreams, Travis. You, with your magazine-cover good looks, your kind heart and your bigger-than-life ideas."

He chuckled. "You failed to mention my ego, my bruised ribs and fractured ankle and my control issues."

"All part of the complete package that make you the Bachelor of the Year."

"I'm hoping my reign is over. Someone else can take the crown." Travis gestured toward the beasts grazing in the pasture. "What about this? Took me all last night to paint those signs."

AJ started to giggle.

"What's so funny?"

She smiled and pointed.

Once again the bison had shifted position and the signs read "Amanda Rowe. Will you." The last bison had completely shifted so her sign faced away from them.

"Cattle. Cattle would have stood still for me." He got down on his knees, took her hand and reached into his pocket and pulled out a blue velvet box.

"What's that?"

"A ring. What did you think it was?"

"Try to be patient with me. I told you that I've never had a boyfriend before."

"And if I have my way, you never will." He popped open the box with one hand.

AJ gasped at the diamond solitaire inside. "It's a diamond. And it's huge. I don't wear diamond rings."

"Yeah, and you don't dance, and you don't dream. I remember. I remember." He sighed. "We're going to start working on turning all your don'ts into dos."

"But rings can get caught on fences or hurt the horses."

Travis shook his head. "AJ, you're making this a whole lot more complicated than it needs to be. Now, hush for two minutes, will you?"

Her eyes rounded.

"Please."

"Yes, boss," she murmured.

"Amanda Rowe, I'm head over heels in love with you. I have been since the day you walked onto Big Heart Ranch, even though I didn't know it at the time. Will you marry me? There's no one else I want to dream about the future with."

"What about my job on the ranch?" she asked.

He groaned and slowly got to his feet. "Are you asking for a raise?"

"No, a promotion."

His head jerked back. "To what?"

"I'm thinking foreman."

"I ask you to marry me and you want my job?"

"I'm in a position to negotiate today. This sort of leverage doesn't happen very often."

"You can have any job you want, including mine."

"No. I don't want your job. I want us to share the position. Partners. Forever."

"Forever?"

She nodded.

"Does that mean yes?"

AJ looped her arms around his neck. "I love you, Travis. I didn't think I'd ever find a man who I loved more than my horse, but then you came along."

"You love me more than Gus?"

"Yes." She pulled his head down to hers. "Please, kiss me."

"What about this ring?"

She held out her hand and he carefully slipped the ring on her finger. AJ grinned. "Now could you kiss me?"

"Yes, ma'am."

As his head lowered to hers, she put a hand on his lips. "Um, Travis, it's after hours." She pointed to the camera. "Are we being filmed?"

He chuckled. "Yeah, I guess we are. Wave at the camera, sweetheart." Raising a hand, he grinned and hammed it up. "The staff will be seeing this on their phones right about now."

"I can only pray they don't put it on the internet," she said.

Travis doubled over laughing. "I am never going to live this down with Tripp and Dutch. They'll be giving me grief about this all summer."

She shook her head. "We're just one big happy family here at Big Heart Ranch, aren't we?"

"Yeah, we sure are." Travis took her hand and tugged. "Come over here. The camera can't see us and I can kiss you to my heart's content."

AJ smiled and followed him.

Could all her dreams that she didn't know she had be coming true? Well, this was certainly a start.

* * * * *

If you loved this story, pick up the first book in the BIG HEART RANCH *series from beloved author Tina Radcliffe:*

CLAIMING HER COWBOY

Available now from Love Inspired!

Find more great reads at
www.LoveInspired.com

Dear Reader,

Welcome back to Big Heart Ranch. Big Heart Ranch is located in the fictional town of Timber, Oklahoma, located near the real city of Pawhuska, Oklahoma.

In this second book you'll meet even more of the staff and children of this ranch for orphaned, abused and neglected children, where love and the Lord reign. The ranch is owned and operated by the orphaned Maxwell siblings, Lucy, Travis and Emma.

Travis Maxwell and AJ—Amanda—Rowe have both faced devastating disappointment and heartbreak. It takes a leap of faith for these two characters to trust the path God has set before them. But stepping out in faith and partnering with each other is the only way they can achieve the fullness of what He has prepared for them.

It's much the same for us. Faith is a walk in the dark. The first step is always the hardest.

I hope you'll come back for more stories from Big Heart Ranch. Do drop me a note and let me know if you enjoyed this book. I can be reached through my website: www.tinaradcliffe.com.

Sincerely,
Tina Radcliffe

Get 4 FREE REWARDS!

We'll send you 2 FREE Books plus 2 FREE Mystery Gifts.

Love Inspired® Suspense books feature Christian characters facing challenges to their faith... and lives.'

FREE Value Over $20

Get 4 FREE REWARDS!

We'll send you 2 FREE Books plus 2 FREE Mystery Gifts.

Harlequin® Heartwarming™ Larger-Print books feature traditional values of home, family, community and most of all—love.

YES! Please send me 2 FREE Harlequin® Heartwarming™ Larger-Print novels and my 2 FREE mystery gifts (gifts worth about $10 retail). After receiving them, if I don't wish to receive any more books, I can return the shipping statement marked "cancel." If I don't cancel, I will receive 4 brand-new larger-print novels every month and be billed just $5.49 per book in the U.S. or $6.24 per book in Canada. That's a savings of at least 19% off the cover price. It's quite a bargain! Shipping and handling is just 50¢ per book in the U.S. and 75¢ per book in Canada*. I understand that accepting the 2 free books and gifts places me under no obligation to buy anything. I can always return a shipment and cancel at any time. The free books and gifts are mine to keep no matter what I decide.

161/361 IDN GMY3

Name (please print)

Address   Apt. #

City   State/Province   Zip/Postal Code

Mail to the **Reader Service:**
IN U.S.A.: P.O. Box 1341, Buffalo, NY 14240-8531
IN CANADA: P.O. Box 603, Fort Erie, Ontario L2A 5X3

Want to try two free books from another series? Call 1-800-873-8635 or visit www.ReaderService.com.

*Terms and prices subject to change without notice. Prices do not include applicable taxes. Sales tax applicable in N.Y. Canadian residents will be charged applicable taxes. Offer not valid in Quebec. This offer is limited to one order per household. Books received may not be as shown. Not valid for current subscribers to Harlequin Heartwarming Larger-Print books. All orders subject to approval. Credit or debit balances in a customer's account(s) may be offset by any other outstanding balance owed by or to the customer. Please allow 4 to 6 weeks for delivery. Offer available while quantities last.

Your Privacy—The Reader Service is committed to protecting your privacy. Our Privacy Policy is available online at www.ReaderService.com or upon request from the Reader Service. We make a portion of our mailing list available to reputable third parties that offer products we believe may interest you. If you prefer that we not exchange your name with third parties, or if you wish to clarify or modify your communication preferences, please visit us at www.ReaderService.com/consumerschoice or write to us at Reader Service Preference Service, P.O. Box 9062, Buffalo, NY 14240-9062. Include your complete name and address.

HW18

HOME *on the* RANCH

READERSERVICE.COM

Manage your account online!

- Review your order history
- Manage your payments
- Update your address

We've designed the
Reader Service website
just for you.

Enjoy all the features!

- Discover new series available to you, and read excerpts from any series.
- Respond to mailings and special monthly offers.
- Browse the Bonus Bucks catalog and online-only exculsives.
- Share your feedback.

Visit us at:

ReaderService.com

RS16R